The Catalyst

The Catalyst

Nicole Luiken

TREE FROG PRESS
EDMONTON

Tree Frog Press gratefully acknowledges support from the Alberta Foundation for the Literary Arts, the Film & Literary Arts Branch of Alberta Culture & Multiculturalism, and the Writing and Publication Section of the Canada Council. Thanks go to Rudy Kendal for his close proofreading.

Canadian Cataloguing in Publication Data

Luiken, Nicole.
The catalyst
ISBN 0-88967-065-X
I. Title.
PS8573.U534C3 1990 jC813'.54 C90-091226-X
PZ7. L84Ca 1990

Printed in Western Canada by Friesen Printers, Manitoba

5 4 3 2 1

TREE FROG PRESS LIMITED
10144 89 Street
Edmonton, Alberta, Canada T5H 1P7

For Mom, who liked the ending

Table of Contents

1. You Didn't Get Any Wrong! 9
2. I am Darkness 22
3. Trevellyan 38
4. The Most Unlikely Couple 47
5. I Always Know Where You Are 56
6. Earthquake 70
7. The Catalyst 84
8. Two of a Kind 101
9. The Total Eclipse of the Heart 112
10. Unto the Seventh Generation 123

About Nicole Luiken 143

Chapter One

You Didn't Get Any Wrong!

The words on the page wavered and dipped before my eyes. I'm not going to make it, I told myself, I'm just not going to.

I had been fighting off the blackness all day, trying to get through this test and now I wasn't going to make it.

Black anger rose up from within me, worsening an already bad headache. It wasn't fair. Why now? Why not tomorrow or yesterday? There was little question of holding out till the end of the test—I'd be lucky to make it out of the school on my own power.

Bright lights glared down on me. Too bright. Lights that filled my eyes with water and tightened the vise around my head. I've got to get out of here. Soon. But first the test. I supported my head with one hand and with half-closed lids stared at my paper. Gibberish, pure gibberish. I gave up the battle once and for all. What the heck, everyone thought I was a moron anyhow—might as well give them some hard evidence. I stopped trying to decipher the questions, just checking off *(A)*, *(B)*, *(C)* or *(D)* in rapid succession.

Done. My movements clumsy with pain, I stumbled to the front of the classroom, tripping once over a chair leg. I kicked out at it savagely, feeling brief satisfaction in the loud clattering noise it made.

Heads shifted and murmurs broke out around the classroom.

"Quiet, please!" Mrs. Hopkins rapped the desk for effect before turning to me. "Yes?" There was no mistaking the icy tone in her voice. "Did you want something?"

Wordlessly, I handed over my sheet and took grim pleasure from the look of utter disbelief that spread over Mrs. Hopkins' face.

You can't be done yet! Her thoughts were transparently clear. *This is the school board's latest Comparative Intelligence Quantification test! It takes hours to complete, not minutes!* She took pains not to show her amazement, saying coolly, "You may sit down now, Medusa." She drew out my name as if it offended her.

I didn't move. I couldn't. The anger in me began to grow.

"Sit down!" Mrs. Hopkins stared at me from behind steel-rimmed glasses. I could almost hear the clickety-clack of her thoughts. *Impertinent girl! We shall see what the principal has to say about this!* "Sit down!" she repeated more loudly.

The whole class was looking on now. I could feel their eyes, sharp and unfriendly, digging into my back. I said one word. "No." It was all I could manage.

The teacher's mouth dropped open, giving her an uncanny resemblance to a fish.

She would have said more, but the pain in my head chose that moment to increase to an unbearable level. Barely keeping the cry of pain from my lips, I pushed past her rudely. I had to get out of here. Now. The door slammed behind me, but no one followed.

The hallway was an indistinguishable blur, and I wobbled down it like a drunken man, clutching at the lockers for support. Pray to heaven everyone else was safe in class and not roaming the halls with me. I was dangerously near the edge now—one word, one look—and I would go over.

Dark. I must have dark. The world, even behind my closed eyelids was white with brilliance. Operating entirely on memory—and something else, my own kind of inner radar—my hands followed the lockers to a small closet just off the Chemistry lab, and gropingly found a doorknob. One twist and I was inside.

Here was blackness, soothing relief that my eyes literally drank in. The painful whiteness in front of them gradually began to fade, going from one great blur, to several bright spots, to gray, to the black I knew it was.

I stood still even after my vision returned to normal and I heard the next period bell ring. Students began to pour into the Chem lab, banging their books down and making jokes. It was the last period of the day on one of the first nice days of autumn we'd had so far and everyone's spirits were buoyant.

Not so with me. Bad weather was my forte, and darkness my ally. Even here, in such cramped quarters as these, I was comforted by it. Here was safety. I dared not leave it until school was over and all the students gone. My anger was still too close to the surface, my mastery over it too weakened by my prolonged exposure to the light.

There was too much light here, period. The old itch to travel found me. Maybe it was time to move on, to another town, to another school. This time one by the sea. Yes, the sea.

I was sure of that somehow. If I listened hard enough I could almost hear the pounding of the surf.

I stiffened suddenly. Someone was coming. Coming here. The footsteps I could hear were not just the footsteps of a teacher walking down the hall or some student late for class. This person was coming here, to this closet, and unless I acted fast they would find me. The hairs bristled on the back of my neck; I did not wish to be found.

The closet had a second connecting door to the Chem lab, and through it I could hear the Chemistry 30 class busy with an experiment. I glanced at the door only once before making up my mind. After all, I needed only to duck inside for a moment and then duck right on back out. I took a gamble and stepped inside, closing the door behind me.

I blinked painfully in the sudden return to light, peering around through slits before deciding that my headache wasn't going to jump out and bludgeon me again.

I saw a typical science room full of black-topped counters equipped with sinks. As yet, no one had noticed me—they were all too busy at their separate lab stations, measuring solutions into graduated cylinders. Someone would have soon, but something else demanded their attention.

At the back of the classroom, I had the best view in the house. And that was all I could do—watch. There was no time to shout a warning, no time for anything but caught breath and congealed horror.

It started with a simple spark, visible for one-hundredth of a second before the whole counter went up in a blazing ball of fire. The girl doing the experiment recoiled, dropping the beaker in her hand.

Some kind of flammable liquid must have been dumped down the sink at one point because that caught fire as well, and—faster than thought—jettisons of flames burst out of all the sinks around the lab.

More beakers fell, fracturing to slivers on the floor and splashing acid. Screams rose higher than human voices should. Some students were just voices, their bodies hidden by viscous black smoke; others were highly visible and aflame.

That was when the first of the explosions started.

I alone stood motionless as broken glass and test tubes rained down around us. The sun caught the glass and refracted into dozens of miniature rainbows, playing over the bent heads of the rest of the students. No shard cut me, and I was not afraid.

One girl looked up and screamed above the tinkling of the glass. Blood was oozing from a cut on her forehead, and her hands were scorched from the explosion ... but that wasn't why she was screaming. I recognized the horror in her eyes from days gone past and knew full well what sight had put it there. For a moment I stared back with a fierce hatred of my own before turning tail and running pell-mell.

The crowd in the hall checked me. The chaos was almost as bad outside the Chem lab as inside. The fire alarm was on, and students from all over the school were milling about in the hallways—all chattering excitedly, all cramming nearer for a closer look. I pushed back and was fighting my way to the exit when a strong hand clapped me on the shoulder.

"Medusa Noire! I suppose I should have known." It was the principal. My eyes flashed resentment, but his hammy hand remained on my shoulder. "Did you just come out of the Chemistry lab?"

I hesitated, unsure of what would happen if I said yes. However, he had no time to waste waiting for me to reply. I was firmly steered to one side and instructed not to move an inch until I'd been checked over by the medics. Others soon joined me, including the girl at whose experiment the whole thing had started. She was in a state of shock, repeating over and over, "But I didn't light a match! I didn't!"

By the time the ambulance attendants got through with the injured people and around to pronouncing me perfectly healthy, the hubbub had subsided considerably. School had been let out, and reporters were busy snapping picture after picture of the blackened lab. The TV crews hadn't arrived yet, but I felt sure they would.

I picked up my jacket and made my way to the front entrance, neither bothering to put it on nor collect my various homework assignments. I'd had more than enough of school for one day.

One lone reporter waited at the bottom of the steps, his hair wind-ruffled, his collar askew. I summed him up at a glance: obviously someone new to the job, called in as a last-minute replacement. "Hey, Miss?" he called. "The name's Russell. I'm a reporter from the Clapton *Tribune*. I'd like to ask you a few questions."

And I'd like to rearrange your face, I told him silently.

He pressed forward eagerly, but fell back in a hurry when he got a good look at me. He hadn't been on the job nearly long enough to become hardened to such stark ugliness as my face.

Still, he recovered rapidly and began to fire out questions. "How close were you to the blast when it exploded? What did the doctors say about your face? Are...."

I could almost see the headlines in his mind. "GIRL'S FACE HIDEOUSLY SCARRED IN CHEMISTRY CLASS EXPLOSION" accompanied by a picture of me, Hideousness personified. This could be his first big scoop, and a raise might even be in the making. There was only one problem: it wasn't the school's fault. Or mine either. I was just the lucky person who happened to have been born with a face like a Mack Truck.

"I wasn't hurt." I clattered down the steps two at a time, my head bent supposedly against the wind. In truth, I just didn't want to have to look at him. I was awfully sensitive about my looks and prone to punching out anyone stupid enough to remind me.

"You weren't hurt?" Trust a reporter to keep on ferreting away for the facts, picking at the scab until it gushed blood. "But you were in the blast? You walked out of a room full of flying glass without a scratch? You must feel incredibly lucky."

Incredibly lucky. I'd heard those words before and I disagreed with them even more violently now than I had then. I whirled around so suddenly that he nearly smashed into me. "There's no such thing in the world as luck!" I spat the words in his face. "Now, buzz off!" I didn't wait for a reply, didn't answer when he called out asking for my name, just walked.

The sun was gone now, buried behind a bank of dark clouds and that suited me just fine. The people I passed on my way to the circus grounds paid me no more attention than I paid them. That was what I liked best about cities, the sense of anonymity. Nobody here would stare.

Our Gypsy caravan wasn't parked in the roughest place in Clapton nor the seediest, but the unpainted, tin-can appearance of its various motorhomes fit right in with the shabby surroundings. I headed straight for the shiny, red fortuneteller's tent. Mine was the after-school shift and Zsa would be getting impatient. The sign, sewn over a hole in the fabric, still read Madame Rosa, but she had been dead almost from the moment I arrived from the orphanage four years ago. I could still see her clearly: the white hair tucked up into a scarf turban-style, the cheeks and mouth rouged. But her eyes had been kindly, unflinching as they looked at my face, and for that I would always remember her.

Madame Rosa had been the one to bring me to the caravan for she had the Gift, the Second Sight, and had recognized a kindred spirit in me. She had known she was dying and had picked me as her successor. Zsa might be a more true-blooded Gypsy than me, but her powers were limited. She got along mostly by shrewd judgment and knowledge of people. She was glad to let me take over afternoons and occasional evenings, freeing her to catch up on things like the laundry and the latest episode of *Dallas*.

Our business was mostly palm and tarot readings. We did have a crystal ball at one time, but it had been cracked during one move or another and never replaced. Today the fortunes came to me in focus, a legacy of the migraine from school. Nothing better for the sharpening of extrasensory perception than a teensy-weensy little half-ton steel block sitting on your head.

Zsa, middle-aged and moled, without her Gypsy scarves, greeted me in Romanee, the language of the Gypsies. The explosion was sure to have been on the radio, but Zsa made no mention of it and neither did I. Things like that were better left unspoken.

My mood improved drastically with the falling of night. This area of the city was not well lit, and low-hanging clouds effectively shut out the rest of the light. I stayed up well into the wee hours past midnight, just staring off into space and listening to the even snoring of Zsa from the other side of the partition. I've never needed much rest, and in truth these hours of sitting alone refreshed me better than twice the amount of sleep.

The light awoke me. Zsa had learned long ago that I could sleep like the dead through wake-up calls and shakings, but awoke immediately to even the tiniest bit of light. I snapped off the light and groggily began to get up. I hated all mornings when there were twelve or more hours of daylight to get through. The shorter days of winter were a joy to me, the summer a nightmare I tried not to think about.

This day I dreaded even more than the others. Yesterday's explosion would be on everyone's lips, and that was something I could do without. The Comparative Intelligence Quantification test results would be in as well, but I preferred not to think about that either.

Mrs. Hopkins' class was third block of the day, right after lunch, but she couldn't even wait that long. No sooner did I set foot in the school than she beckoned me from her office. "Medusa, I'd like a word with you."

I hesitated fractionally before following. I squared my shoulders. Might as well get it over with.

"Please, take a seat. There's something I'd like to discuss with you," she began formally, pausing to close the door firmly behind her. "I think you know what I'm talking about. You've been holding out on us."

I kept quiet, a kind of defiance in my choosing to remain standing, my hands curled into fists. This was not going to be pleasant. I smoothed out my face into the picture of blandness.

My very coolness seemed to irritate her. With angry movements Mrs. Hopkins reached into her desk drawer and produced a stapled paper. "This is what I'm talking about, Medusa." Again that slight distaste over my name. She thunked it on the table in front of me.

Surprise, surprise, my C.I.Q. test. I winced. The test of all tests, and I'd checked off the letters at random. I'd probably scored somewhere in the vicinity of a home-grown squash.

"Well, aren't you going to look at it? Or do you already know what you got?" Mrs. Hopkins was quivering with rage, and her voice was hard as she asked, "Did you really think you could get away with it? Did you honestly think you could pass yourself off as a moron?"

I shut my eyes, trying to tamp down the anger before it got a chance to take root. I was going to stay calm. I was not going to get angry. I was—

"Listen to me when I speak!" Mrs. Hopkins banged a fist down on her desk, and my head jerked up, my eyes wide and starey. "I've checked with the other teachers and you're scraping by in their classes as well. We both know you could be pulling nineties."

That got my attention. Nineties? I'd never gotten above a seventy-nine percent in my life, and that was on an open book test in Grade 4. Bombed a silly Quantification test I might have done, but I was hardly straight A's material to begin with. "I don't know what you're talking about," I told her calmly.

This time Mrs. Hopkins shoved the test in my face, almost shouting, "You have a perfect C.I.Q.! You scored above genius. YOU DIDN'T GET ANY WRONG!"

I didn't believe her—not then—and took a longer look at my test paper. Silently I flipped through all three sheets, scanning the columns of check marks. When I did speak it was haltingly, "Are you sure—are you very sure?" There had to be some mistake somewhere. The wrong name on the paper, an extra hundred carried over to the total. Something.

Mrs. Hopkins sounded more weary now than angry, and she drew a hand across her eyes as if to wipe away sleep. "I've checked it over a dozen times at least. It's all here in the handbook." She pushed the yellow Teacher's Guide toward me almost pleadingly. "You can check for yourself if you want."

I made no move to take the book. Carefully, I reviewed in my mind the day I'd taken the test, and the reason for my high score stuck out like a sore thumb. Migraine. Checking off answers at random. My improved fortunetelling when I got home. It all fit, just like all the other times, numerous other occasions when I'd been accused of cheating and had to stand here like this struggling to explain. It never got any easier, and Mrs. Hopkins reaction was typical.

"Well?" she surveyed me coldly, arms folded across her chest. "What do you say now?"

What to say indeed. I almost didn't bother, almost walked right on out the door without saying a word in my defense. Didn't I know, better than any, that as far as proof went I had less than a leg to stand on? So, I began by apologizing, and cursing myself while I did it. "I'm sorry you've gone to all this trouble, Mrs. Hopkins," her eyes narrowed, and I took a deep breath, "when it's all for nothing, really. I don't suppose anybody ever told you where and how exactly I live?"

Mrs. Hopkins stiffened as if to say, "Spare me the sob story, kid. I don't buy a word of it."

I sighed and began anyway. "You see, I live in a Gypsy caravan, and after school I run the fortunetelling tent." I looked down at my hands and made myself go on. "I have the Gift. Extrasensory perception to you. I had a headache yesterday afternoon, and I couldn't finish the test on my own, so I just started checking off answers. I guess I must have accidentally used my ESP." My words tumbled to a halt. I looked up pleadingly at Mrs. Hopkins' face. It remained hard and unyielding.

"Come now, Medusa. Can't you think of anything more convincing than that?" Her words were deliberately chosen to cut. "I expected better of a genius."

The blood began to beat in my ears. She didn't believe me ... wouldn't believe me if I swore it on a stack of Bibles. Nobody ever believed me.

"Speak up, Medusa. I can't hear you!" Her words vibrated in the still air of the office. "Speak up!" she commanded.

But I no longer had anything to say.

The phone on her desk began to ring, short angry rings that would not be ignored. When Mrs. Hopkins turned to pick it up, I quietly left the room.

Mrs. Hopkins was two steps behind me, shouting dire threats, but the phone started up again, to be joined by another in the next office. I smiled and kept on walking. Served her right.

But my smile didn't last long. There were more urgent matters to be attended to. The pounding in my head had started again, the pressure building with leaps and bounds. If there was one thing I was sure of, it was my own temperament and its irregularity. Any and all bursts of anger had to be properly channelled or else ... one day I would lose control completely and never get it back.

I headed straight for the exit. The contents of my locker could rot; I was going to get out of here now while the going was good. Zsa or Leo could come for my transfer papers in the morning, but I was through. Tomorrow we'd move on. Although Leo was the undisputed leader of the caravan, he had learned to trust my judgment on these things and made sure the caravan could leave on half a day's notice.

The wind, along with a stray leaf or two, hit me slap in the face, and the sun railed down at me. Compromise weather, I'd always called this—neither here nor there, but someplace in between. Not at all like me. My side of the fence was always clearly defined and marked Wrong.

Around me I could sense the usual stares and attention I was attracting. After all, outside of freak shows and reruns of *The Hunchback of Notre Dame,* how often did people see such an ugly person as me? Bitterness clogged my throat.

Two voices off to my right rose loud enough for me to hear. "Who's that?"

"Where? Oh," then in a tone of complete indifference, "you must mean the Battery Killer."

I walked on and some tiny trace memory of mine clicked into place, matching faces to the voices. The second was a classmate of mine, the first was Russell from the newspaper.

My true thoughts, though, were elsewhere. The name of the next town had just come to me—Lorelei—and, true to my vision, it was by the sea.

Chapter Two

I am Darkness

"I'm telling you, I lost it," insisted the girl with the snapping black eyes and fashionably short haircut. "One minute it was there and the next it was gone." She widened her eyes innocently and the class sniggered.

The teacher looked rightfully skeptical; the girl's last assignment had been chewed up by the family dog under decidedly suspicious circumstances. It was obvious even to me that she simply hadn't got the work done and was trying to wriggle out of losing marks.

"You seem to have been misplacing a lot of things lately," the teacher said ponderously. "Perhaps the docking of ten percent will encourage you to be more careful next time."

"Excuse me," I said loudly, speaking entirely on impulse. The whole class turned to stare at me. In the three months I'd been here, this was the first time I had spoken voluntarily. Even now I came close to retracting the words. "Are you talking about a yellow binder with a Daffy Duck sticker on the inside cover?"

The girl blinked. "Uh, yes. How did you know?"

In fact I hadn't known until a picture of it popped into my mind. "I saw some guy take it on you and hide it in his locker. He'll probably turn up on your doorstep tomorrow morning and return it to you. Personally." I placed deliberate emphasis on the word.

The girl stood there dumbfounded. She was more vivacious than pretty, but a surprising number of boys seemed more than willing to walk her to and from class.

Everyone laughed and the teacher said teasingly, "Looks like you have an admirer though I wish he would be slightly more conventional in his courtship! The ten percent is hereby revoked. Okay now, class, open your textbooks to page 101 and take it from there."

And so class went on. When the bell rang, I was the first up out of my seat and through the door. I had little desire to be questioned about my spur-of-the-moment story or to receive a pat on the head for it. To me the matter was closed, and I suspected the brown-haired girl would forget me within hours.

I was proven wrong at lunch the next day. She fell in behind me in the lineup, wrinkling her nose at the food choices. "What do you think is safe to eat?" she asked cheerfully.

I responded totally without thinking, "The chili's good today, and the apple pie." I knew the words were wrong the moment they came out of my mouth. The girl's face took on an interested look.

The line ahead of me moved, and I rushed to close the gap and start dishing up, ending the conversation. I heaved a silent sigh of relief. The girl was sharp—no matter how late she chose to hand in her assignments—and was therefore to be avoided at all costs.

I quickly paid and headed for my usual spot. One side of the cafeteria was all windows, and only in those seats directly in front of the kitchen could the sunshine be avoided. The girl behind me followed, setting her lunch tray down in the seat across from me. Some of my consternation must have shown on my face because she laughed. "Don't look so surprised! I just wanted to thank you for saving my hide in English the other day. My marks aren't all that great, and I really couldn't afford to lose that ten percent." She paused, "My name is Nancy Jean."

"I'm Medusa," I mumbled, since it seemed expected of me. I was growing more nervous by the moment. Why didn't she just go away? Talking to me in the lunch line was one thing, sitting down with me was quite another. I was uncomfortably aware of the curious looks we were attracting, and it didn't help matters any that most of the starers were Nancy Jean's own friends.

For a couple of minutes there was silence as we both attacked our food with gusto. Me, to prevent having to talk, and Nancy Jean because, as I was later to discover, she was always hungry.

Nancy Jean finished first, wiping her mouth with a napkin and leaning back with a satisfied look on her face. "Mmm, that was good!" She studied me carefully. "Do you work in the cafeteria?"

"No." I turned startled eyes to her face.

"Hmm, 'curiouser and curiouser,' as the saying goes." She took another swig of her chocolate milk. Setting it down, she said casually, "You know, I really didn't have that essay done, and I was sure grateful when you vouched for my story. I figured you must have seen my Daffy Duck binder somewhere. Then a funny thing happened; last block of the day I really did lose it. I go home, write out my essay on different paper and think real hard where I could have lost it. And *then* do you know what happened?"

The question was rhetorical, but I knew the answer anyway. A slow shiver made its way up my spine as she began to tell me.

"This morning, just before school, Bill Howard shows up on my doorstep. He found something of mine and wanted to return it. You'd never guess what it was." Her brown eyes looked into mine evenly. "He had my yellow binder." She paused to let that sink in.

I kept quiet, rationalizing. I would have to be careful here not to give myself away. Nancy Jean might suspect, but she didn't *know* for sure ... and she mustn't know. The same instinct that had gotten me into this whole mess told me that.

"Anyhow," Nancy Jean went on abruptly, "it so happens I like Bill, and I let him walk me to school, but I'm beginning to get a very weird feeling about all of this. And most of all about you." Her face was dead serious. "I've asked around, you know. You've been here since mid-November. It's early February now and nobody knows a thing about you beyond your name. Medusa Noire. Lorelei is not exactly your big town, and I've lived here all my life. I know the way any new kids are immediately welcomed by a barrage of questions. You never say anything, do you? You wait until someone asks you straight out and they feel rude. Well, I'm asking you now, Medusa Noire, how'd you know Bill would take my binder and return it to me, even before I lost it?"

I immediately went on the defensive, my eyes cool and wary, studying Nancy Jean's face. This wasn't the first time I had been boxed into a corner. I doubted it would be the last. The truth was out of the question, of course. Back at the orphanage I'd learned the hard way how hypocritically people act when confronted with the truth—the real truth of the matter, not their own particular distorted version of it. And so I compromised. Liar was not a label I cared for. "Maybe I overheard him planning it with his friends or they overheard me telling you and thought it sounded like a good plan."

Nancy Jean grinned suddenly, the smile transforming her whole face. "And maybe I'm the King of Kazoo! Fine, don't tell me. I've always had an urge to follow in the footsteps of my namesake, Nancy Drew!"

I didn't have the slightest idea who she was talking about. It must have shown because Nancy Jean laughed again, this time in disbelief. "You don't know who Nancy Drew is?"

"I just moved here," I snapped. "I haven't gotten around to memorizing the phone book yet."

Nancy Jean laughed all the harder, and my mouth clamped tightly shut. The beginnings of anger were rapidly stirring to life inside me. I jumped up to leave. I didn't like being laughed at.

Nancy Jean smothered her mirth, catching at my sleeve. "I'm sorry," she said contritely, still a hint of laughter in her eyes. "It's just that Nancy Drew isn't a real person. She's this girl detective in some books, and I've had this fixation on her for ages. The same names you know. Everyone else knows about it and humours me."

"Sure," I avoided her eyes and studied the space just over her shoulder. The boy and girl two tables down were having a bang-up fight, and I felt like joining them. "Well, I gotta go now." I headed purposely out the door. The bell rang and I left her behind in the crush of people that followed, but I felt oddly anxious all day as if I hadn't yet seen the last of Nancy Jean.

One day passed, and then two, without more than a glimpse of her in English or at lunch. Thursday was sunny and the glare made my walk home decidedly unpleasant. I'd been forced to take a window seat in my Social class and the constant light had given me my usual headache.

I walked swiftly, keeping to the shadows, but I had gone no more than a half a block when I stopped short, the hairs prickling on the back of my neck. Someone was watching me. Blast these small towns! In cities the passersby were prudent enough to keep their eyes to themselves. I speeded up.

I crossed the street, but the feeling of eyes persisted, even growing stronger, until finally I ducked round the stucco corner of the nearest building and grimly waited. I had come to the conclusion that someone was following me. I'd eluded muggers in the big cities before, and there was no way some smalltowner was going to follow me anywhere.

Sure enough, I could hear running footsteps as my tracker panicked at having lost me. My anger swelled, and I reached out and roughly grasped the jacket of whomever was tailing me, my second hand already bunched into a tight fist. Startled eyes met mine, mouth parted in a silent O shape. I let go of the jacket in confusion.

It was Nancy Jean.

"Oh, hi, Medusa! I was just looking for you." She grinned saucily, not at all alarmed. "But I guess you already know that, huh?" She rubbed her shoulder ruefully. "So much for my great Nancy Drew detective act! Is this where you live?" She successfully changed the subject by pointing to the two-story apartment house we stood in front of.

I could've lied. In fact I wanted to, but after the smallest of pauses I shook my head. "No. Come on and I'll show you." I tramped down the mud in the back alley.

Nancy Jean kept up a running commentary on the way there about everything and everyone. I responded to none of it, slogging on ahead. The caravan wasn't more than two blocks away, but I bypassed it in silence. It was too cold to put up the fortunetelling tent outside, so Zsa had rented us a stall at the nearby Farmers' Market & Trade Fair where we set up the tent instead.

"In here." I pushed through the first set of doors and bent to undo my boot laces with fingers stiff from the cold, expecting Nancy Jean to follow suit.

She, of course, did nothing of the sort, choosing instead to stand there staring, mindless of the puddles she was making on the linoleum. Her very-small-child-in-a-candy-store look paid tribute to all the hard work we'd done the week before taking down the Christmas decorations in favour of an early Valentine's Day scene. Valentine's was one of our better fortunetelling seasons, though it called for a lot of the same old questions.

"Stay here," I instructed her. Nancy Jean nodded, and I vanished into the changing room opposite.

Long practice made my donning of the Gypsy scarves and earrings take no more than a minute, and the switch with Zsa went off without a hitch. I peeked out the specially-made eyeholes in the tent and waited. True to my expectations Nancy Jean had not stayed put and was already working her way down my row.

Her purse was out and the crafty look in Mrs. Atkins' eye told me plainer than words that "We've got a live one here, folks!" Nancy Jean must have a soft spot for cuddly little stuffed creatures and all the other knickknacks being sold in the booths. It was a good thing the fortuneteller's tent was only fifth down the line or she would be milked clean before she got here.

Ten minutes later, giggling a little, she came through the front flap into my tent. It was dark inside, and were it not for two old-fashioned glass lamps none of its red velvet interior could be seen. Not only did the poor lighting create an eerie atmosphere and hide the worn places in the tapestry, but when I croaked, in true Gypsy fashion, "Cross my palm with silver," my customers always jumped a foot in the air.

Nancy Jean was no exception, her head jerking towards the sound of my voice in unmistakable fright. I rose up from my cushions with grace and glided forward, hand outstretched. "Cross my palm with silver and have your fortune told."

"Oh! Of course." Nancy Jean began to dig into her purse, then her head came up with a delighted smile. "Medusa, is that you? You just gave me the scare of my life!"

Annoyed at how easily she'd seen through my disguise, I ignored her, repeating, "Cross my palm with silver."

"Why not?" Nancy Jean laughed. "I've always wanted to have my fortune told." She dug in her purse and came up with a handful of change. "Is this okay?"

It was indeed okay, in fact generous. Had she given less I would have remained there, hand outstretched. My fingers closed around the coins, and I unobtrusively pocketed them. "Be seated." I gestured vaguely towards the various red throw cushions on the other side of the table. "What kind of a reading do you wish?"

Her answer was prompt. "Crystal ball."

My expression didn't change. "Regretfully, the crystal is in need of recharging. May I suggest a palm reading?"

"By all means."

In the same smooth tone I inquired further, "Long-range forecast or short?"

Nancy Jean smothered a laugh. "Sorry, it just sounds like you're talking more about the weather than my life."

To this, I made no response.

She held out her hand. "Short-range please."

The shape of her hand and the lines crisscrossing it told me many things about her personality itself, but nothing that I didn't already know or hadn't guessed beforehand. That wasn't really what I was looking for. I closed my eyes, mentally reaching out. The headache helped as always; a quick impression of a picture formed almost immediately. The red velvet around me receded.

I spoke in low, almost chanting tones—barely aware I was speaking, so engrossed was I in the drama unfolding before me. "You will be getting a surprise soon. A pleasant one, I think. A boy from your past will come back into your life." I frowned, my hand going up unconsciously to my forehead. The picture was growing disturbed instead of gradually coming into focus like most. I struggled on, wrestling with the strong emotions gripping me. "He is tall and blond and—" I cried out suddenly as light totally blotted out the picture of the boy, and opened my eyes to the near darkness of the tent.

Nancy Jean was leaning forward, listening intently. "Tall, blond and what?" she questioned eagerly.

This time I had no answer. "Please," I rose abruptly with none of my earlier smoothness. "If you would leave now." I felt drained and somehow frightened by the experience. It had been oddly personal this time, as if it was not only Nancy Jean's future but mine as well.

She left, albeit reluctantly, and other customers came, but they did not fully capture my attention—perhaps I read their fortunes the better for it. Often when I really concentrated on seeing something, nothing would come to me, but when I was asked a question out of the blue I would blurt the answer without thinking. Like Nancy Jean's binder or the chili.

Friday was Semester Break, and the next week started off with all the usual bustle of timetable juggling and the confusion of trying to find the right classes. Once I caught a glimpse of Nancy Jean waving to me from the other end of the hall. She seemed excited and tried to push her way forward through the crush of students, but the bell sounded, and in the end she gave up and just waved.

I consciously tried to avoid her. It had been an insane impulse of mine to show her the fortunetelling tent. I hoped that the less she saw of me, the less likely the story would go round the school. Being tagged as a Gypsy fortuneteller, even if it were true, was the kind of hassle I could do without. The ones who didn't tease or beg me to have their fortunes told for free would look upon me as just that much more of an oddity: that I could not stand.

Valentine's Day was coming up, and volunteers from the Students' Union were everywhere, handing out computer match-up forms and persuading people to come to the dance.

The Home Ec room was always too bright, so when the bell rang I did my level best to be first through the door. This time I was, and Nancy Jean, with a Students' Union card pinned to her sweater, was waiting to nab me.

"Medusa!" Nancy Jean's voice held genuine warmth, something I was unused to hearing, and for a moment it rocked me. Most people who knew me well enough to call me by my first name also knew enough to avoid me like the plague. I wasn't ... safe.

"I haven't seen much of you lately. I don't think we have any classes together this semester, do we?" Actually we did, Mr. Farr's Accounting class first thing in the morning, but after hiding out in its back corner for days I wasn't about to say so now. Nancy Jean rushed on in any case. "And of course there's this business about the dance. Are you going?" Her eyes searched mine in that disturbingly friendly way.

I backed up, one of the hunted. "No." Other students streamed around us, hurrying to their lockers.

She looked almost hurt. "Why not?"

"I don't want to." It was a sullen sort of answer to give—especially when Nancy Jean was the only person who'd gone out of her way to be nice to me in the three months I'd been here—but as always, the words came out bluntly. They were also the truth. I'd never been to a dance in my life, not even a piddly school dance like this one, and I had no intention of ever going.

Nancy Jean tactfully changed the subject. "Anyhow, I wanted to tell you, that prediction of yours? About the tall, blond-haired boy I once knew? Well, it came true and—"

"Shhh!" I pulled her over to one side, looking around with panicked eyes to see if anyone else had heard. I thought not.

"What is it?" Nancy Jean started to say, but I quelled her with a look. I stared into her eyes intently, almost hypnotically. "Don't talk about that. I don't want anyone to know. Nobody, okay?" I shook her slightly.

"Okay," Nancy Jean nodded her head rhythmically.

"Good." I started to rearrange my books and walk off.

She snapped out of it almost immediately, grinning her widest. "But if I keep my mouth shut, you have to come to the dance, okay?"

My alarm system went on the alert. I DIDN'T want to go. My mind told me clearly how just standing at the sidelines watching the couples dancing would be enough to infuriate me, but what else could I do? I was trapped ... and knew it. "All right, I'll go." I sighed, but I hadn't said how long I'd be there. A few quick dances and I would disappear.

"You won't be sorry." Happily, Nancy Jean scribbled my name down on a list and gave me a form to fill out. "Hand it in to your home-room teacher when you're done with it."

I shifted my books to the other arm and took it. I dreaded the questions it was likely to have, like: *What do you do in your spare time? (A) Read (B) Watch TV or (C) vegetate.* My answer would have to be C as I did very little of the other two, reading only when forced to and unable to get interested in Zsa's soaps.

As it turned out, the questions were a lot simpler, having to do with two or three clear-cut choices and no hypothetical situations. There were questions on height and colouring and what personality type you considered yourself. There was even one on whether you enjoyed school. That one was the easiest to answer; I filled in the *(D) hate it* block without hesitation.

Only one question had the power to hurt me and that was the one that asked: *How do you rate your looks? (A) beautiful/handsome (B) cute (C) plain (D) ugly.* I checked off *(D)*, taking savage satisfaction in knowing that compared to me, no one else even qualified.

I could see the shock in Zsa's eyes when I told her where I was going that Friday night, but she wisely said nothing and turned back to her darning.

Hoping they would have the lights romantically dimmed allowing me to fade into the shadows, I dressed entirely in black. I washed and brushed my hair with little result other than some undesirable bushiness and set off praying no one would notice me, and most of all, that no one would laugh. I could stand a lot of loud music, but even the tiniest giggle had been known to set me off.

I got there a little on the late side, just when they were doing the announcements, which was good because even the girl taking my money hardly looked at me.

Not surprisingly, it was Nancy Jean up at the mike, announcing, in between whistles and applause, the ten most likely couples. "And the tenth couple is ... Jamie Fischer and David Hunter!" The cheers swelled again as two computer-matched-up teenagers blushingly appeared from opposite sides of the red-and-silver-streamered gym and took their places together on the podium.

Nancy Jean cleared her throat. "Now for the moment you've all been waiting for. The Unlikeliest Couple is...."

For a second, time froze—my hands clenched into fists, my face suddenly drained, because I knew ... knew whose name she would call.

She started to speak, but the P.A. system suddenly whined at a pitch so high people had to cover their ears. Nancy Jean quickly flicked it off and yelled above the hub-bub. "The winners are Medusa Noire and Simson—" His last name was swallowed up in a tumultuous cheer. Whoever he was, it appeared, he was not unknown to the crowd, and the crowd not unknown to him.

He was tall and blond and smiling from ear to ear. On his way up to the stage, he called out jokes to his friends and generally clowned around. Being thrust into the limelight didn't seem to bother him a bit; in fact, he reacted as if he'd been born there. I could instantly see why we had been chosen the Most Unlikely Couple with my dark aspect and his fairness. His hair was so white that it hurt my eyes, but I couldn't've looked away from him if I'd used a sledge hammer. I recognized this boy—Simson she'd called him—almost immediately as the "old friend" in Nancy Jean's palm reading ... but that wasn't what held my eye. Neither was it his extraordinary good looks. It was something else, some sense of *déjà vu* my ESP was reacting to.

I had not been aware of Nancy Jean moving, but suddenly she was at my elbow towing me to the front. I didn't want to go, didn't want to see the golden boy's face when he caught sight of his prize. Nancy Jean pushed me into the light.

That silenced the crowd, or shocked it rather. I knew I was ugly and I'd accepted the fact long ago, but that didn't stop something within me from crying out in pain. The light hurt me, its sharpness combined with the whispers in the crowd slicing right through me. It showed up the pallor of my skin and hole-in-the-blanket eyes, cruelly highlighting the sharp angles of my face and hideous nose. It was cruel, the crowd was cruel, and cruellest of all was Sim's face, for it showed pity.

Then he let loose a wild yell. "Come on, let's party!"

Nancy Jean reacted quickest, starting the stereo up so fast she scratched the record. She dimmed the lights as well, and I blessed her for it. I needed darkness to recuperate in. Only darkness was kind. I started to turn away, but someone caught at my hand.

It was Sim. "Hey, you can't go yet! The party's just starting."

For me the party had already ended, but I allowed myself to be pulled onto the dance floor. I said nothing, not trusting myself to speak. He was doing all this out of pity, of course—I could read it clearly in his face. I watched my feet, moving awkwardly, out of sync. I stepped on his foot once and looked up miserably, apologizing with my eyes. "Sorry."

"That's okay." His voice was soft and near my ear. "Hey girl, loosen up. Forget about all those other people. Just do as I do, and let the music do the rest."

Obligingly, I opened my ears to the song and tried to relax. Sure enough my movements did seem freer, though I couldn't help but flinch every time the big light flashed our way.

The song ended. Disappointed, I started to walk away. He'd been polite and I'd had my dance; I might as well leave now.

"Wait!" Again that hand on my elbow. Sim smiled disarmingly. "Care to dance another one?"

I couldn't help but smile back, totally forgetting the row of uneven teeth I was exposing, and returned to the dance floor. The song was faster this time, more abandoned. Its very beat got into my blood as I danced in and out of the dark and the no-longer-cruel half-light. It was then that I saw Sim's eyes change when he looked at me. It wasn't pity they held now. Was it admiration? Fascination? I didn't particularly care, but the peculiar jolt I felt upon first seeing him increased with the tempo of the music. Vibrations filled the air.

The next song Sim didn't even ask to keep dancing; he just held me there with his eyes. For me the other dancers ceased to exist. There were only the two of us and the rhythm flowing around us.

We stayed on the dance floor practically all evening, going to the refreshment stand once, and then only briefly. I knew we were attracting stares, and for once, recklessly, I didn't care. Let them look, let them talk! Tonight was mine and I hugged every minute of it to myself, as fiercely as a lioness protects her cubs.

The dance was drawing to an end. The deejay began dragging out all the old hits, the slow smoochy numbers, and Sim sighed, "Aha! A slow one at last!"

I smiled widely, as I had been intended to. "Why, are you getting tired?"

"No," Sim smiled, and I caught my breath. It was the smile of an angel and yet....

The song started up, the beat pulsing in time with the strobe light, in time with our hearts. Sim's arms were around me, and he was gazing into my eyes as if he never wanted to stop. I knew I didn't.

A stray phrase caught my ears and quivered deep down inside of me. "ONCE UPON A TIME THERE WAS LIGHT ... AND NOW THERE'S ONLY ... THE DARK." It struck a chord and, unaccountably, I shivered. Then the chorus swelled on great waves around us: "THE TOTAL ECLIPSE OF THE HEART."

I stopped dead in the middle of the dance floor and Sim stopped with me. Something was teasing the outer reaches of my Second Sight. I grasped at it, but it slid through my fingers, leaving me with only an overpowering sense of horror. "No!" Mine was a cry of despair against I knew not what. "No, no, no!" My hands dropped from Sim's shoulders to come up and cover my ears, but the song would not be shut out.

Bam! Bam! B-B-B-Bam-bam!

Dozens of the red heart-shaped balloons overhead began to pop, slowly at first and then quicker—louder—like gunfire.

I fled the room and its motionless, staring inhabitants. One thought filled my mind: *I've got to get out of here.* I tore through the halls like one possessed; the song floated after me on the air, the singer's husky voice straining over the chorus, "THE TOTAL ECLIPSE OF THE HEART." I slammed the door behind me. It was stormy outside, snowing heavily with raging winds, and I had no jacket. But I was not cold, and I did not stop running.

Someone was behind me, plowing through the frozen slush and ice with little regard for anything but speed. I could hear only the footsteps, but I knew it was Sim, and I knew he would not catch me.

Gradually the sounds slowed, and I sensed him falling. "Wait!" he called.

I hesitated, saying nothing.

"You've got to tell me!" His voice was desperate, hoarse almost, "Who are you?"

I knew he was not referring to my name. My answer came from deep within me. "I am Darkness," I said, not knowing why I said it. Then, suddenly frightened, I turned and fled into the night.

Chapter Three

Trevellyan

Snow fell all that night and the next day. And the next. The wind howled, battering against the walls of the motorhome until it shook, curtaining off the rest of the world with a blanket of purest white. It was a storm that Lorelei hadn't seen the likes of in over twenty years and probably wouldn't again in that many years to come.

I loved storms, loved their fierceness and the sense of isolation they brought. I had little fear of the cold. While everyone else was safely curled up inside, I was out in the thick of things letting the elements do battle for me. There was a lot on my mind, not the least of which was Simson.

A million times I asked myself why I had made a fool of myself by running out into the storm. But there I stopped because I did know why—I knew that if I had to do it all over again, I would've done the exact same thing. The vision had been too harsh a warning to ignore.

Monday morning, when the storm was over—a doubt had never crossed my mind that the storm wouldn't be over by Monday—I'd have to try my best to pretend Friday night had never happened. It shouldn't be too hard, I reasoned. After all, before Friday I hadn't so much as bumped into Sim in the halls. My lip curled up into a sneer—who was I kidding? Chances were, once Sim saw me in full daylight, he'd take off like a bullet from a gun. The thought hurt me strangely, and I purposely repeated it to myself: *like a bullet from a gun.*

Monday came earlier than I'd wished, along with the sunshine. The glare from the snow was extremely painful to my sensitive eyes, forcing me to wear sunglasses to school that morning. They were doubly useful as a sort of disguise. The last thing I wanted to do was reattract attention to myself after that awful moment up on the stage when the Unlikely Couple was announced.

I saw Sim twice that day. Both times he saw me, and both times I managed to avoid meeting him: the first, through a temporary power failure that halted everyone around me, giving me time enough to duck into the girls' washroom; the second, when a fight broke out among several boys between us. I went home that day feeling reprieved.

Unfortunately the feeling didn't last much longer than the snow did. The next day Nancy Jean joined me in the cafeteria lineup, butting ahead of several people to do it. "What's good today?" she inquired breezily. We might have been old friends from the way she talked.

"The hamburger," I replied mechanically. I supposed I was stuck with her—there was little chance of a second power failure and I doubted that would stop her anyway.

She followed me to my usual table and watched intently as I liberally doused my hamburger and fries with ketchup. She showed no inclination to eat her own. "He's been asking about you, you know." The words were blunt.

"Who has?" I kept my voice casual, but my hand holding the salt was shaking, and I think she saw it.

"Come off it, Medusa!" Nancy Jean's brown eyes snapped. "You can cut the crap. We both know I'm talking about Sim! He says you're avoiding him. Why?"

I carefully returned the salt shaker to its usual place before replying. "Maybe I don't want to see him."

Nancy Jean gave an unladylike snort. "And maybe I'm niece to the Queen of England! Look, I'm not blind, you know, and neither's the rest of the school. We all saw you dancing last Friday and how you pulled the Cinderella act and disappeared on the stroke of midnight!"

It was twenty after twelve, I protested silently, and if you had seen what I had seen ... my mind shrank from recalling it.

"Well?" Nancy Jean demanded righteously.

I kept very still. The rage was building within me again, and while part of me taunted myself *(That's right, Medusa. Get angry, blow up all over the place. Take the easy way out just like you always do.)*, the other part knew just how little real control I had over it. My head began to pound in a way I remembered only too well, and the lights hurt my eyes. "Well, what?" I stuck to playing dumb; it had served me well in the past.

"Arrgh!" Nancy Jean ground her teeth in frustration. She picked up her tray, adding cuttingly, "Exactly why Sim is wasting his time asking about you is beyond me!" She slammed her way over to the another table at the far end of the room.

Coolly I picked up my fork and began to eat again, remotely surveying the people around me. One girl's tray got up-ended on her dress, and someone else was having a hard time getting the ketchup out of its bottle. He gave it an extra hard thump and half the bottle emptied at once. I smiled thinly to myself; this place was nearly as bad as the orphanage.

That set the mood for the rest of the day—like it had been at the orphanage. My temper was dangerously close to the surface, the black clouds hovering over my head almost visible. My headache was getting worse instead of better.

Zsa took one look at me when I got to the Market, and immediately backed off. We exchanged no words of greeting other than, "Sure you want to go on today?" to which I nodded. Perhaps the dark would cure me.

I had my eyes closed when a pair of footsteps told me my next customer had arrived. "Cross my palm with silver and get your fortune told," I intoned, fluttering the whites of my eyes for effect.

The change was cold. A person from outside, I surmised, not a regular with a table in the market. It was a nickel short of the dollar I expected, but I let it do the usual disappearing act, still without a word from my customer. I stubbornly refused to open my own eyes, saying only, "Palm, please."

The hand itself was warm. I traced its four lines—life, head, heart and fortune—with my thumb. Light slashed its way beneath my eyelids and I dropped the hand as if it were a hot coal. I KNEW this hand of old, knew well the lines engraved upon it.

"Trevellyan!" I snarled, taking a huge step back against the red fabric of the tent. My hands involuntarily curled into claws.

My eyes were open now, and what they saw made me stop, appalled. Staring back at me from out of an unnaturally pale face was ... "Sim?" I questioned. My ESP had never failed me before. I felt like the object of some inner tug of war.

The deep-rooted feelings of hatred—and, yes, fear—were still with me in full force. "I don't understand," I wailed.

"I am Simson Trevellyan."

The pressure inside my head increased abruptly.

"And you are?" he asked.

I blinked stupidly. They were the last words I was expecting to hear. Totally forgetting my ridiculous Gypsy get-up, I couldn't understand why he didn't recognize me. "I? I am Medusa."

I just had time to catch the merest glimpse of his expression—not surprise, but a curious I-should-have-known—before the red walls of the tent came collapsing down around us. It happened quickly, an accidental bump to the pole no doubt, and down it went.

The first thing I saw after crawling out of the tangle, between blinks, was Sim's tousled blond head. The static had done amazing things to his hair, but that wasn't what stopped me, my breath catching in my lungs. On my hands and knees, I stared at him and he stared back, some flash of ... recognition? ... binding us together.

"I always did say that tent would fall down one day." It was Mrs. Atkins speaking somewhat smugly from my elbow.

Neither of us jumped. Sim's blue eyes showed only quick amusement, which came close to bubbling into genuine laughter when she added, "It's a wonder nobody got hurt under all that heavy cloth."

"A real wonder," I agreed politely, rising up off my hands and knees with as much dignity as I could muster. I turned briskly away from Sim and addressed the crowd that had gathered. "Now then, if a couple of you would help me clear this up ... ?"

It only took a few minutes to fold up the tent and rescue the lamps and various cushions. I was careful to keep my eyes on the red of the material, resisting the force that pulled them towards the pair of pale, pale hands near mine. I tugged fiercely at a bit of drapery where it stuck. It's a matter of self-preservation, I argued to myself, that was all. Look at him and you're sure to fall flat on your face.

All the same when the hands disappeared from off the fabric, I followed soon after, murmuring excuses to Mrs. Atkins. Zsa could put up the tent in the morning; I was out of here.

I stepped out briskly, walked two steps and came to an abrupt halt, as if suddenly reaching the end of an invisible leash. All the hairs rose up on the back of my neck—and not from static electricity either. "You can stop hiding now," I said, my eyes still glued straight in front of me.

Sneakers squelched, and Sim materialized at my side. He was grinning. "I can see it's going to be almost impossible to sneak up on you."

My lips twitched at the corners in the beginnings of a smile, but I hastily damped it down. This was not the place—not with Mrs. Atkins and fellow crewmen peeking out the windows at us. I began to walk, and Simson agreeably kept pace along beside me. We walked in a not-uncomfortable silence. I had nothing to say that could be safely translated into words.

It felt good to be walking in this way beside him. I didn't even mind the sunlight that danced and sparkled on the hoar-frosted tree limbs. In fact, I was sorry to come to the park bench and the questions that must be asked. And answered. I started, turning and looking at him for the first time since that awful moment when he'd said he was Trevellyan. "Why did you wait for me?"

Sim's answer was quick and easy. "Why, I wanted the rest of my fortune told, of course!"

Of course. For a moment I almost felt pity for him. Always the quick reply, the lazy smile, the parrying of any thrust that came at all close. In a way, he was just as handicapped as I was, just as sensitive, only I tended to react in anger instead of covering everything up with a joke. For this reason my tone was almost gentle as I asked, "Is there any question in particular you'd like answered?" It was part of my Valentine's Day routine, the girl's cue to ask about the boy she liked.

"Yes." There was a decided twinkle of mischief at the back of Sim's blue eyes. "At the risk of repeating myself, who are you?"

I froze. The voice wasn't hoarse this time, but for a fraction of a second I was back out in the snow and the cold after the dance. Behind it, there was the same need to know, despite the warmth of his smile. The sun caught me full in the face, and I blinked rapidly, my eyes watering. "I don't know."

That took him by surprise, knocking his grin momentarily askew, but he soon bounced back. "Why? Are you an amnesia victim?" he probed lightly, ready to back down at the first sign of distress.

"Try an orphan." My voice was bleak. "They found me on the road complete with a name tag: Medusa Jobyna Leila. I made up the last name—Noire is French for black," I volunteered, surprising myself. I'd planned on telling him I was an orphan, nothing more. Or alternatively not even that.

There was no real answer to that, and Sim didn't even try. One of his hands reached out and took mine. Now that I wasn't trying to "read" his palm, it was a comfort, and when he gently squeezed mine, I returned the pressure before drawing it away.

"I've still got both my parents and all of my grandparents. Doesn't seem quite fair somehow." Sim's blue eyes studied the horizon.

"And cousins galore?" The pull I'd felt immediately towards him at the dance reestablished itself. I suddenly wanted to know everything about him.

"Funny you should ask that, because amazingly I have none. Mom was an only child and Dad's side is even worse. Every generation, one male heir is born to carry on the Trevellyan name." Sim was smiling now, kidding. I didn't smile back.

The hairs on the back of my neck bristled like an animal on the defensive. The bitter taste rose up again in my throat and I had no idea why. I barely managed to choke back the words, "Of course, everything else might be left to wither and die, so long as the Trevellyan name would be carried on!"

"What is it?" Sim switched his gaze back to me. "What's wrong?" I kept silent. What could I say? That I hated his last name? Hated it as irrationally as—I shivered abruptly and kept on shivering.

"Cold?" Sim was instantly concerned. He got up and offered me a hand. "It's just above freezing, I ought to know better." His glance slid over my rather threadbare coat with a contempt he couldn't quite disguise.

But that was pity, the last thing I wanted from him. The flame of anger jumped higher within me. The very last thing! I didn't stop then to think what it was I did want, merely saying with my old stiffness, "Any other questions?"

"Just one." In the face of all warnings, verbal and non-verbal, Sim proceeded, "Why did you run out on me in the middle of the dance?"

I was not prepared. The gray of the day around me was torn from my eyes a second time to be replaced with the black of darkest night. For some thirty seconds I remained there, the song throbbing on waves around me: "THE TOTAL ECLIPSE OF THE HEART." My sense of inarticulate horror escalated with every breath.

"Hey!" It was Sim's hand on my shoulder that pulled me out of it. "Hey, Medusa, are you all right?" His face held unmistakable concern, but I gave myself no time to dwell on that, rushing into excuses. There must be no more questions, either from him or from me.

"Look, it's getting late and—"

"You have to get home?" Sim finished smoothly.

"Yes."

"Great. I'll walk you." He matched steps with me.

I stopped. "No, you won't." I strove to keep the panic out of my voice.

"I won't?" He stopped too, the grin still in place.

"No." I didn't mince my words.

"Okay, but don't think this is the last you're going to see of me."

Sim's face was unnaturally serious this time, his eyes direct, so that I almost asked, "Is that a threat?" I had to swallow hard to keep from giggling.

"No, that's a promise." Sim chucked me gently under the chin before turning and sauntering off.

I was left standing there, mouth slightly open and eyes dark with inner turmoil. Whether Sim realized it or not, he'd just read my mind.

Chapter Four

The Most Unlikely Couple

Any previous ideas I'd had about quietly becoming Sim's girlfriend—for it seemed I was, although I couldn't recall being asked—flew out the window at about noon the next day.

It wasn't that Sim purposely set about to attract attention, but he was the golden boy and people just naturally watched. A few gaped when he waited for me at the school entrance, and a few more nudged elbows when he walked me from class to class, but there was also a general feeling of disbelief. They had to be reading more into the situation than there was. They had to be. Not until we entered the cafeteria together did the serious speculation start.

As Fate would have it, at just that moment there was a tiny pocket of silence, rare to lunchrooms and schools in general. All eyes swung our way. In the back room somebody dropped some pots and pans that clanged repeatedly before coming to a standstill. Everyone jumped except for me. I was not surprised; I'd already gone through this once before, breathed it and lived it in the dark tunnel of my Second Sight.

My nerves tightened under the barrage of so many eyes. I almost balked, but Sim held firmly to my hand. I hated being the centre of attention. It made me feel like some circus freak show.

Fortunately Sim seemed to understand. "Chin up," he whispered and led me safely around to a table by the window. Despite the light and the orange plastic tablecloth, my heart warmed at the sight of it. It was a table for two only. "Be right back." Sim left me to join the hot-lunch lineup.

The flow of lunchroom conversation resumed its course. Now the whispers started, along with the sidelong glances. Rumours and speculations flew thick and fast as the night of Valentine's Dance was rehashed. That made it easier for me: it's difficult to remain frightened for very long when you're getting angrier by the minute. With a suddenness that turned every eye in the place on me, I got up and jerked the curtain across my side of the window. No sense in getting a headache as well. I left Sim's side of the table in sunlight. Shade made Sim's face look gray. I reaffirmed my earlier judgment—Sim was born to the light.

He returned shortly with two plates of limp-looking spaghetti. Sim looked at me in amazement as I dug in without hesitation. "How can you do that? I usually bring along my own food tester for places like these."

I shrugged. "Early training, I guess." There hadn't been a lot of choice in the menu at the orphanage. You ate what was put in front of you, and that was that. I had little use for food anyway beyond a source of energy. "Food's food."

Sim grimaced. "I don't know if that's exactly the category I would place this stuff under." He prodded it delicately with his fork. "It looks like the cook lost his toupee somewhere in the process."

"Or like snakes," I agreed cheerfully, winding the strands around my fork and taking a big mouthful.

Sim's eyes turned sly. "Or both."

I chewed slowly, warily. There was some significance here, I knew it. A head of snakes, writhing and twisting. Now who had a head of snakes?

Sim's smile grew, and he started to lift his plate.

Click! Now I knew! Medusa of Greek mythology had a head of snakes. Sim raised his plate higher as if he were going to dump the spaghetti on my head. I chuckled low in my throat, "You wouldn't!"

"Oh, wouldn't I?" The devilish gleam in his eye was impossible to mistake now.

"No." The words came naturally. The words of a prophet. The playing was over. I attacked my spaghetti once again and Sim started more cautiously on his. We must have made quite the spectacle, laughing at each other's attempts to keep the spaghetti on the fork and pausing every so often just to look in each other's eyes.

Nancy Jean stopped by once, just long enough to say "Hi" and to give me the thumbs-up sign behind Sim's back. She tactfully left right away although I could tell she was bursting with curiosity. And if her smile was a trifle smug, like one who has successfully played the Matchmaker, well, bully for her.

I polished off my plate first, and Sim generously offered to share what was left of his. I took him up on the offer and laughed, saying impulsively, "Do you remember that one scene in *Lady and the Tramp* when they were both eating from the same plate of spaghetti?"

"And they ended up eating the same noodle? Oh yes," Sim nodded gravely. "Why else do you think I picked it?" He smiled so angelically that I couldn't help but smile back.

I let him eat the last noodle, which he did with considerable ceremony and the appropriate facial expressions, but I couldn't laugh. All around us was silence, and when we got up to leave, there was only a handful of people left in the room, just pretending to eat. Their eyes closely followed our every movement.

The short walk from our table to the door represented to me all the danger of a minefield. I left the navigation to Sim, and he skillfully threaded a way between the tables, dispatching a smile here and there, but not stopping any longer than to say "Hi." And we almost made our escape, too. Only at the last table, one girl, sensing her prey was about to get away, forcibly detained us with an iron grip on Sim's jacket. She had peroxide-blonde hair, dyed eyebrows, and I hated her on sight.

"Why, hello, Sim!" she cooed. I resisted the urge to shred her face with my nails. "Remember me? Rachel? It's been a long time. I hadn't even heard you were back till this morning."

Liar, I accused her silently. Liar, liar, liar.

Sim made some polite rejoinder and made as if to go, but that apparently wasn't going to be allowed. "Please sit down. There are absolutely oodles of things I want to ask you," she purred, sending him a smile worthy of a barracuda. She was about as hard to read as an Archie comic.

Sim remained standing, eluding her questions as best as he could. The flame of anger burned ever brighter inside of me, alarming me so much that I tightened my grip on Sim's hand with all my strength. I had to get away now, before—

"And you?" she smiled charmingly.

Too late I realized the question was directed at me, and I could only numbly mutter, "Uh, um."

So Rachel repeated the question. Slowly. "Do ... you ... like the ..."

My ire rose. How dare she talk to me as if I were some great big stupid child!

"... school? Oh, God!" Her exclamation could be heard two tables away.

"What is it?" Sim asked, startled.

"Yes, Rachel, what is it?" I mimicked with malicious intent. Of course I knew perfectly well what was bothering her. So would Sim if he happened to look at my face.

For a moment she seemed incapable of speech—a decided improvement in my opinion. "It's ... it's your eye!" she got out at last. "It ..."—*shudder*—"it wanders. I think I'm going to be...." She got up suddenly and lurched across the room towards the exit.

Sim sent me a Do-you-know-what-that-was-all-about look. I just shrugged. A lady knows there are some things best kept secret.

We spent the rest of the noon hour sitting in a doorway to one of the classrooms quietly talking. Somehow that was something we'd done very little of in our previous meetings, and I hung shamelessly onto every word Sim uttered. He had a talent for making the most routine of incidents sound funny, and I found myself laughing more than I had in years. Perhaps ever.

The bell rang much too soon. For a few minutes longer Sim and I didn't move, waiting for the crush of bodies to abate. I watched him out of sight before donning my sunglasses and making my leisurely way to Accounting class. We had gone over our whole semester's schedules only to discover we had absolutely no classes in common, which probably explained why we had missed seeing each other before the Valentine's Dance.

I was late, of course, but I didn't particularly care. I felt higher than a kite, practically floating my way in through the door, but I came down with a decided thump. Bypassing all rules of greeting, the teacher laid into me, his words heavy with sarcasm, "Decided to join us today, Medusa? Wipe that smile off your face and sit down!"

I didn't move. My face turned red—with anger. I never blushed. I didn't pause to wonder why Mr. Farr attacked me when he generally made little fuss over lates; I had learned early on that there were a great many things a cute, clever child could get away with that I could not. Staying up an extra half hour, getting two scoops of ice cream instead of one—the list of injustices was as endless as it was petty.

"And get rid of those sunshades! Can't you tell it's winter around here!" Mr. Farr's words held barely concealed contempt.

So I removed them, keeping my eyes fastened on Mr. Farr with his bald domed head and nonexistent eyebrows. I hated my eyes; they were malformed like the rest of me, and I wondered if he had ever really seen them before. My pupils painfully contracted to almost nothing, and I could feel my left eye beetling around in its socket, crossing and uncrossing itself with a mind all its own. Strangely, it only did so in the face of light, never in the dark.

Someone—I later found out it was Nancy Jean—pushed me into the nearest desk. I suppose that saved me, as Mr. Farr then wisely redirected his attentions to school matters. I sat statue-still through the entire length of his precious class and cared not a whit.

Once Nancy Jean whispered to me "to at least *pretend*" I was working, and I went so far as to pick up my pencil, but my grip was so strong it broke between my fingers. The snap sounded loud in the classroom, heads turning to stare, but it frightened me most of all. It meant I was barely in control. I tried to calm myself by counting to one hundred, and I succeeded in part. I was no longer angry with Mr. Farr, but I was primed and ready for the next spark.

I have big ears, comparable to Mr. Spock's, only lopsided. They hear too well for their own good. Somewhere around number forty-seven I became aware of some whispering and giggling from the other side of the class. I tried not to listen—I really did—but the harder I tried to shut them out, the louder their voices seemed to get. They were talking about me, of course. For half the class I endured, waiting and waiting for the bell to ring. Come on, you stupid thing, ring!

The harassed voice of the school principal came over the loudspeaker instead. "The bell is temporarily out of order. Please go to your next class." Slowly, deliberately, I picked up the books I hadn't opened and left the classroom. The two whisperers were ahead of me. I hadn't once looked their way, but their guilt might as well have been emblazoned on their foreheads. I knew.

They must have felt my eyes on them from behind because they shut up awfully fast, the short, frizzy-haired girl hurrying her friend down the hall in a flurry of skirts and feet. My locker was down the other hall, and I would have turned the corner in another second. *Would have,* you see, because the other girl—the blonde with curly hair and a face like an angel's—just couldn't resist getting in one last spiteful shot.

In a high, mock-pitiful, carrying voice she said, "Poor girl, she really is a moron if she thinks that Simson Trevellyan might actually be interested in *her.*" The sweet musical laugh trilled out.

Only nobody laughed with her. Everyone within earshot had been watching my face and they fell silent, afraid. People still opened lockers and chatted down the other end of the hall, but, as Nancy Jean would swear later, nobody so much as breathed at my end.

Rage, sheer black rage, overwhelmed me. It had been a long time since it had gotten out of control like this—months even. I had come a long way since the days in the orphanage when my blowups were frequent, sometimes twice a day. Too bad my emotions hadn't matured with me; they were still as primitive as ever. The blonde girl had struck out at me without provocation and she would be made to pay. In my own terms.

The anger radiated out from me in waves, with a strength that both exhilarated and frightened me. The force of it was physically present, literally slamming students and teachers alike into the walls and out of my way. I started towards her.

The blonde was scared now. Her little joke had backfired and she was woefully ill-prepared to take the consequences. She was alternately screaming for help and heaping insults on my head. The fact that she is still alive today only goes to show that I had long ago stopped listening to what came out of people's mouths and instead was concentrating on what went on inside their heads.

I knew her name now—Clarissa Gail—and the names of everyone in her family and her grade-point average. I also knew why she had said what she had. She was jealous. She wanted Sim for herself.

At that point any other person would have stopped and spared her, for I also knew with absolute certainty that Sim had not so much as looked her way. Nonetheless, there was no pity in me, and I was already half out of control.

I backed her into a corner and shook her till her teeth rattled. I was strong for a girl, even stronger in my anger, and Clarissa wasn't much competition in any case. She got in one swipe at my face with her fingernails that did more damage to her manicure than my cheek. Ignoring that, I got hold of her hair, dragged her over to the fountain, and turned the water on.

Her yellow curls dissolved like jello and her eyes were mascara-smudged when I let her come up for air. Her cotton-candy pink dress was water-stained, maybe even ruined. Still I felt no pity. Her Daddy was filthy rich, and I doubted she would ever want to wear it again, no matter what its condition.

Huddled miserably against the wall under the fountain, Clarissa was sobbing. I wondered if she knew exactly how lucky she was. My fist itched to blacken her eye, but I knew myself well enough from my days in the orphanage to resist. Once I started punching, I wouldn't be able to stop. I'd probably broken more kids' noses and school equipment in the years I lived there than had happened in its whole forty-year history.

I headed for the front doors. Behind me I could hear the school administration suddenly spring to life and fish Clarissa out of her puddle. She was crying in earnest now and saying, My Daddy this and My Daddy that. He was going to sue the school and have me locked up. I had little fear of that; there were too many witnesses around to swear I was provoked for Daddy to pull it off—even if he was a member of the school board. I'd been expelled before, and there was no heavier punishment.

More likely, we'd both get a good talking to, and Clarissa would go home to her Daddy, but I had no intention of sticking around even for that. Right now I needed to be alone—to put some space between me and the rest of the world.

Chapter Five

I Always Know Where You Are

It was as unseasonably warm out as it had been unseasonably cold the night of the Valentine's Dance. There was mud everywhere. Personally, I preferred the high winds and darkness of the storm. I put on my sunglasses and set off to find myself a hideyhole. The physical exhaustion that always followed one of my outbursts was beginning to make itself felt.

My feet knew the way. Around one corner and the squat blue school was out of sight, two corners and only the rising of smoke denoted the town. A hundred paces more and I was where I wanted to be. The cliffside.

It stretched up and up and up, weather-seamed rock bare of all colour, with me hidden in its shadow. The snow hadn't melted here, and a harsh wind swept in from the wide expanse of blue-gray sea. Below me the waves pounded, grinding ice against the rocks with a power and rhythm that exhilarated me. In a strange way I lived through the force of the ocean just as I had gloried in the fury of Friday's storm.

I sat there and watched the endless waves for I don't know how long. I kept very still, letting myself be absorbed into the picture. I never really said it, even to myself, but I was waiting. Eventually my diligence was rewarded.

I knew it was Sim before I even turned around. I couldn't speak—my throat felt raw—and I didn't try. I made room for him on the rock and we both sat and stared at the surf for a long time. There was no need for words just then; the silence was enough; it remained unbroken except for the intermittent cry of a gull.

Neither did we speak of Clarissa though I was positive that Sim had been fully briefed on all the details. Clarissa, once dealt with, meant nothing to me. A week from now I would barely recognize her name. My anger was like that, terrible while it lasted, but fleeting.

Eventually, he turned and faced me, gently removing my sunglasses. "I want to see your eyes," he explained huskily. I looked back at him unflinchingly, without fear. My ugliness would not drive him away. The light dazed me and tears automatically swelled in my eyes.

"What's the matter?" A tiny frown etched itself across Sim's forehead.

I didn't like his expression. Sim was meant to smile, and I spoke quickly, brushing a hand across my eyes. "It's nothing," I denied. I was not yet ready to tell him of my fear of light. He was born to the light and could not possibly understand.

Compelled, I asked the question that had been plaguing me, "Why did you come here?"

The offbeat Sim of last afternoon would've answered cockily, masking his true feelings behind a smile. But this Sim, the Sim from the dance, answered truthfully, "I needed to see you."

My heart lurched within me. *Needed to see me*. Such a strong phrase compared with *wanted to*. Yet the questioning had to go on. I had to know for sure that this strange link I felt with him was not entirely one-sided—an aftereffect from my ESP and anger at Clarissa. "How did you know I would be here?"

For a second Sim looked confused, trying to remember, then his confidence returned and his slow, devastating smile reached his lips. Brilliant blue eyes locked with mine. He replied simply, "I always know where you are, Medusa."

From that moment on, I no longer hated my name. It had sounded ever so much more than a name when he was saying it.

And then we kissed. It was a mutually shared kiss, not just one person kissing the other. It would have been perfect were it not for the deep sense of *déjà vu* that went with it. More than Fate, I could almost hear the faint whisper of a dying woman saying, "At last! Just a little longer and I will be Truly at Rest."

The words, floating through my mind, startled me so much that I opened my eyes and the kiss ended. The echoes soon vanished, fading out once I focused on Sim's face again.

"Thank you," I said.

Sim's eyes blinked in surprise. "Why?"

Something within me twisted. "Because," I answered shortly, "you didn't look as if you thought you'd suddenly caught some incurable disease." Amazingly, I had been kissed before, once or twice by boys whose names I couldn't even recall. Their kisses, though, had been pale shadows of Sim's, and the only thing that I remembered was the identical look of shock on their faces. They'd backed away hastily, mumbling apologies and every time we'd met thereafter their thoughts had been all too plain to read. *I kissed that?! Thank God no one saw!*

"Hey," Sim said softly. The unpleasant memory faded as if it had never been, and I smiled back at him. "School should be out by now. We really should be getting back."

I didn't want to go. Everything within me cried out against leaving this magical place, but Sim was right—it was time. Wordlessly, I let Sim pull me to my feet, and we started walking back. I gathered up my battle armour along the way; I was fully aware I was going to need every bit of it.

By the time we got to the school the buses were gone, and only a handful of stragglers were left. Sim had badminton practice from 3:30 until 5:00 and I had my fortunetelling: obligations neither of us wanted to be held to. And so, we stood together at the top of the steps for a moment longer making plans to attend tonight's movie.

The hairs on the back of my neck prickled defensively. Someone was watching us. I shifted position slightly and let my eyes roll over to the far corners of my vision. I detested being spied upon.

He was easy to spot, leaning lazily against the stone of the building. His face was heavy with flesh, though his body was more massive than fat. He made little pretense of not staring, but in his eyes there was something of an animal's low cunning.

I had a brief, unsettling premonition. Flickers, Zsa called them, and the name seemed appropriate in this case, as if a candle in my mind suddenly flared up and then glimmered out. I saw enough to warn me, a hideous metallic hate, but not enough to see what of.

"Sim," I cut him off mid-sentence and pointed to the boy's now retreating back. "Who is that?"

Sim switched tracks smoothly, apparently getting used to my sudden changes of subject. "That's Ralph, all-round tough guy and school bully." Something hardened in Sim's eyes, became flintlike as they continued to follow Ralph's progress. "Why do you ask?"

The question was framed almost casually, and I responded in a like manner. "I always like to know whose nose I'm breaking." In my mind I heard again the solid snap of splintering bone.

"What?!!"

Sim's exclamation pulled me out of my vision with a thunk. I stared at him in dismay. I hadn't meant to say that, but it was too late to retract the words now. My mouth stayed closed, my eyes wary, as I watched for his reaction.

After a moment's struggle, Sim chose to treat it like a joke. He whistled low under his breath. "That's quite the tiger you've chosen to take by the tail, Medusa. He's at least twice your size ... and mean, too. I hope you're not serious."

I was dead serious, but I chose to shrug instead. "Maybe."

"Why pick on him anyway?" Sim turned curious eyes in my direction.

I avoided his gaze. "I'm the fortuneteller. Remember?"

Sim looked relieved. "Oh yeah. That."

I looked at him sharply. The way he said "That" made it sound like a bunch of hooey, but I let it pass. I wasn't about to let myself get dragged into that mess.

Fortunately, the badminton coach chose that moment to show up, poking his head around the gym doors impatiently. "Are you coming today or tomorrow, Trevellyan?"

A spasm of something very much like hate shuddered its way through my body—my hands clenched into fists. There was that name again.

Sim was saying something to the coach so he missed my reaction, turning to me only to say, "Blast it anyway! What's your phone number? I'll call you around six, okay?" He was already backing his way towards the doors.

"No go," I told him, struggling to sound natural. "We don't have a phone."

"What do you mean you don't have a phone?" Sim was incredulous. Even ET has a phone, his tone seemed to imply.

"I mean we don't have a phone," I repeated more sharply than I had intended. I tried to explain, "I live in a motorhome. We're Gypsies. We wander."

"How often do you wander?" Sim's eyes looked into mine intently. The coach was at the door again, but Sim ignored him.

"Every few months or so," I shrugged. "Whenever the fancy strikes us or the meals get too thin or...." I trailed off uncomfortably.

"Or what?"

I shifted feet miserably. "Or until the situation at school gets so bad I get expelled."

Total silence met that answer. Defiantly I tossed back my black mane of hair, my anger ever ready and close to the surface. Sim, when I dared look him in the face, looked neither shocked nor repelled, but more drawn and ... anxious ... as if the question he was about to ask was of utmost importance.

"And can they? Expel you, over Clarissa, I mean?"

I laughed genuinely. "No. Not even if her Daddy is on the school board!" And caught my breath for fear Sim had noticed my slip. Not once in all this morning's rage had Clarissa mentioned that her father was on the school board.

Sim, however, let out a large breath of relief. "Good."

"See you at the theatre, then." The coach was beginning to look daggers at me, so I turned to go.

"The theatre?" Sim's face showed blank surprise. "I thought I'd come by and pick you up. Where do—?" But I was already down the steps and rapidly moving out of earshot.

The movie playing was a comedy as I had known it would be and a funny one at that. I learned two things that night. One, that Sim preferred his popcorn plain—no salt, nothing—and two, that he loathed the dark almost as much as I hated the light.

A bunch of Sim's friends met us out front, boisterous and rowdy, the "in crowd" complete with school jackets and mile-long lists of accomplishments on their sleeves. Nancy Jean was with them, with a wide-shouldered square-jawed date of her own, looking perfectly happy. Sim plunged into an animated discussion about who would win the Stanley Cup this year while I listened half-heartedly to Nancy Jean's chatter about people I didn't even know.

I felt horribly out of place and almost sick with despair. What was I doing here? I didn't belong. I should be back at home, safely hiding in the fortunetelling tent with a deck of tarot cards for company. Then, just as I was considering excusing myself to the washroom, Sim caught my eye over the shoulders of the others and winked. The tight knot that was my stomach untied itself, and I relaxed. Sim wanted me here; his opinion was the only one that counted. In the end it was Nancy Jean who broke it up by stating she was cold and forcibly dragging her own date off to a front-row seat. "Come on! These two would probably appreciate some time to themselves without you around to butt in."

Wide Shoulders made some retort that had the whole quartet of them laughing and they rapidly passed out of hearing range. That was one thing I'd noticed immediately about all of them. They teased each other constantly, pulled hair, threw popcorn and had a great time. I sincerely hoped Sim didn't expect that from me. I wasn't sure I could do it.

Only Sim didn't really want to talk. We held hands and he concentrated solely on the movie. I knew then, had half guessed it from before when we had always danced directly in front of the spotlight. Sim hated the dark. His eyes never wavered from the screen in the same way that I sometimes stared at the largest dark object in sight. It mattered little what it was, so long as I could look at it and pretend the light all around me wasn't really there. Closing my eyes was easier, but then people were apt to ask questions. Sunglasses were the closest thing to a compromise I had found.

Sim rushed us out of there even before the ending credits started to roll. We rejoined the two other couples and went out for pizza. Nancy Jean told me laughingly that I'd have to get used to missing out on the movies endings because come hell or high water Sim was always out beforehand. He had an instinct about such things.

I vowed to myself then and there that, for Sim's sake, I would avoid movie dates as much as possible. The thought of what effect the light might have on me did not so much as cross my mind.

"Yeesh, but you're quiet!" Nancy Jean eyed me curiously over the booth's vinyl-top table.

I started, pizza halfway to my mouth. "Sorry," I apologized, "I guess I'm just not used to having so many people around." I wasn't used to having friends, period.

Nancy Jean's date smirked. "Don't worry, you'll learn. *Some* people learn too well." He glanced significantly at Nancy Jean.

She wrinkled her nose,"Ver-ry funny," and they were off again.

I leaned back and watched, exchanging amused glances with Sim. This was almost as good as the movie itself.

"Seriously," Nancy Jean said to me a little later when the subject had reverted to hockey, "you aren't mad at me or anything?"

I smiled. "Seriously, should I be? I presume it was you who told Sim where to find me after school."

Nancy Jean looked blank.

So I prompted her, a new urgency in my tone, "About the fortunetelling tent?" *Please say you did, pretty please?* But all Nancy Jean did was shake her head.

"I didn't tell."

A queer, cold prickle made its way up my spine. I had the helpless feeling of forces at work beyond my control. How had Sim known to come there? He had seemed genuinely surprised to see me there, but I had no faith in coincidences.

Without warning, the light chatter of the restaurant faded around me. I was back in that ever-midnight world I'd seen at the dance. The fear was with me again, a horrible suffocating fear that lodged itself in my throat and pulled a blanket over my eyes. I'd seen some awful things before through my ESP, but never anything like this. There was a stillness in the air that I didn't like. It was unnatural and could speak only of death. Cold death, so very, very cold.

"Hey, Medusa, we're leaving! Medusa?" Someone was waving a hand in front of my face. I blinked heavily, and the room gradually came back into focus. It was Sim and he looked worried. "Are you okay, Medusa?"

"Yeah," I nodded, scrambling out from behind the table. "Just fine." However, my legs felt weak, and I didn't like the blast of cold air that met us at the door. Didn't like it at all.

Sim's purring monster of an expensive car started as smooth as silk—then gave a slight hiccup and stalled dead. Sim tried it again with the same result. He smiled in amusement. "You know, this has all the elements of the Sorry-we're-late-but-we-ran-out-of-gas stunt. Only, I assure you, I would have picked a more romantic locale." He waved a hand to indicate the pizza parlor we were still parked in front of.

"I should hope so!" I shot back. My mind was already one step ahead of his. No wheels, no ride home. For reasons I still couldn't quite fathom I didn't want Sim to see where I lived. I wasn't ashamed of it exactly; I'd already told him it was a motorhome—one step up from a trailer, but for now I'd much rather it remained unseen. It was within walking distance, only two lighted street corners away, and I told Sim so. Just not the direction.

He didn't like the idea one bit. We were still arguing over it, when a fancy blue car pulled up and parked directly under the yard light. "Hey, Dad! What are you doing here?" Sim grinned affectionately and jogged over to talk to him. Panic kicked through my veins with a strength that was as frightening as the panic itself. The need to run was overpowering and, used to obeying my instincts, I fled.

By the time I got home my fear had abated, and I went to bed happy, if unexpectedly sleepy. A lot had happened in one day.

Next morning, Zsa had no need to wake me. At 8:06 on the dot a shaft of sunlight hit me full in the face, jerking me awake and upright. For a timeless moment I sat there, heart beating painfully, my eyes seeing only a great blur that was my room.

I forced myself to move around, yanking on jeans and a sweater. Zsa looked at me with something akin to surprise when I stumbled into the tiny kitchenette. Breakfast was still in the process of being made, so I grabbed some bread and the jam and sat down.

Neither of us said a word although Zsa looked as if she might want to. I glared her down both times. Mornings, especially sunny mornings, did not improve my temper. I was not in the mood to be questioned about anything. Still, her curiosity gave me a couple moments unease. She'd shown little sign of it before.

The reason for her curiosity was parked just outside the motorhome door.

I climbed in beside Sim with an odd feeling of acceptance. I ought to have known it was him when I saw the sunlight.

Sim was as silent as I was, revving the engine to life, his only words a kind of triumph. "I always know where you are."

"So you do," I replied. Then, ever so smoothly, we were pulling up to the school and I was getting out. I made no effort to explain my behavior. How could I when I didn't know myself? Sim would just have to accept me the way I was.

For a month we went on like that, dating but not asking questions. It was enough that things *just were*. Neither of us had any wish to pry into either the past or the future though I was prone to visions of both. In the same way, I think both of us were waiting, ignoring but not totally unaware of something building in the air. The imperceptible tightening of a noose, day by day ... and then, quite suddenly, the lull was over and the storm upon us.

It was a gray day out, the clouds low and sullen, the last pockets of snow beginning to melt away and disappear. And I was wildly happy. Happy and free as the wet wind that blew down on us.

"Isn't it a great day?" I breezed over to where Sim was standing in front of his locker buttoning his jacket.

He made a dour face. "Yeah, just wonderful." But we were still under the fluorescent lights and his eyes were smiling as he said it. A couple of the others gave me a strange look but said nothing. Clarissa had not been forgotten yet.

I looked around for Nancy Jean. Of all the group, I knew and liked Nancy Jean the best. She alone was totally at ease with me. She was supposed to be catching a ride home with Sim and I today, being currently in between boyfriends. "Where's Nancy Jean?"

"You mean you don't know?" That was Jill from two lockers down, eyebrows lifted, feigning surprise. She was a friend of Clarissa's and had been cool to me from the start. She had been the one to inform me that Sim and Nancy Jean had been dating just before he left town the first time. Her eyes had been sly as she said it, suggesting that perhaps, now that Sim was back for good....

I said nothing but my eyes didn't leave her face except maybe to cross themselves. Beside me I felt Sim become still as well. He had yet to "see me in action" and I doubted he wished to now.

"She's over by the gym doors talking to some guy," Jill said hastily, taking a half step backwards.

She needn't have bothered; my attention had already switched to the matter at hand. "Some guy" didn't mean a lot with Nancy Jean. She went through boyfriends like some people breathed air, but something within me sharpened at the mention. Minutes later when Sim was ready to go, this same "something" brought me up short before I went round the corner.

I held up Sim too, putting a finger to my lips. Around the corner I could hear voices.

"So you will call me if you notice anything?" It was a man's voice, not that of some high-school boy.

"Oh sure," Nancy Jean's voice was warm. "But I tell you those kind of things happen all the time. Why just the other day I was in the hall and the pay phone started ringing. I answered it and there was no dial tone, nothing. I hung it up and it started all over again with no time for dialling in between. It did that two or three times and then just stopped."

"Really?" the man seemed genuinely interested now, almost torn. "I really do have to run now, but if anything else should happen...." He left the sentence dangling.

"Yeah. Bye." Nancy Jean came round the corner, nearly ramming straight into us. "Medusa! Sim! I wasn't expecting you," she said loudly.

I cringed. He would be sure to hear, and I ... didn't want him to. My eyes riveted themselves to his retreating back. For a second it seemed that he paused and almost turned, but at the last moment changed his mind and walked on. I breathed a sigh of relief and turned away from the door only to discover that both Nancy Jean's and Sim's eyes were trained on me.

I pinned on a bright smile. "Let's get cracking," I said, ploughing my way past them before they could ask the questions in their eyes. There was no real reason behind my hurry and they knew it. Sim especially seemed able to see through my camouflage almost without effort. The thought scared me a little.

I rode up front in Sim's sleek red car only listening with half an ear as Nancy Jean rambled on in the back. Sim laughed and responded—at least superficially—while I stared straight ahead.

Of course it was natural for Nancy Jean to talk about the strange man. "He's researching some kind of supernatural phenomenon. For some kind of book or something." Nancy Jean shrugged. "I didn't quite catch that part."

Book or something. That would fit in. All journalists were supposed to dream about one day writing a book, weren't they?

"Only he had a different name for it—a catalyst, I think."

So what? What did it have to do with me? Nothing of course, and yet ... my instincts told me it could be important to me. And to Sim.

"And this catalyst ... thing ... is able to set off all sorts of chain reactions around it without being affected itself. See what I mean? Real heavy stuff." Nancy Jean would no doubt have gone on with Sim's encouragement, but just then the car slowed to a stop in front of her house.

I snapped out of it long enough to manufacture a smile and wave to her before we were off again.

"You knew him, didn't you?" Sim's eyes were on the road, but I shifted uncomfortably anyhow. His words were calm enough, but they still made me feel about as transparent as glass—a decidedly new feeling for me. It was usually the other way around.

I played dumb. "Knew who?" It might've fooled a hundred teachers in the past, but I had no hopes that it would fool Sim.

He sighed slowly and kept his eyes on the road.

I felt miserable keeping things from him when there was really so little to keep. Just a feeling, that was all. *Yeah,* I jeered at myself, *just a feeling*. And how often in the past had these FEELINGS rung true? Ninety-eight, maybe ninety-nine percent of the time?

This time I was the one to sigh, for I did know who Nancy Jean had been talking to—at least by name and occupation. The new-to-the-game journalist from the Clapton *Tribune,* sent to cover such mundane things as explosions in school chemistry labs.

Russell.

Chapter Six

Earthquake

"Clarissa ever give you any more problems?"

Sim's question threw me off balance. That had happened such a long time ago! "Not a one," I replied cheerfully, "I guess her Daddy couldn't do much after all!"

"Guess not." Sim smiled with me. He tried for a bit of comedy. "Just don't punch out the principal's daughter, okay? They're generally a lot less understanding."

"Tell me about it!" I groaned, sliding further down into the plush interior of the car.

Sim cast me a startled glance while signalling to turn. "You mean you actually punched a principal's daughter?" His mouth was agape with astonishment.

I nodded. "Right on the kisser."

"What'd she say to you?"

My face darkened. For a moment I was back in grade school. The principal had asked me the exact same thing, and my reply was no different now. "Nothing." He'd then gone on to ask if she'd started the fight. He had been a fair man, that principal, but I had guilt stamped all over my face, and several witnesses had already attested to the fact that I'd just walked in and started swinging. And so I'd just sat there, head down, legs swinging—all the time my anger growing in leaps and bounds. My foster parents at the time had been sent for, and I sat like a lump through their questions as well. Shortly afterward I was returned to the orphanage.

"Sorry," Sim's voice broke into my thoughts. I didn't ask what for; I knew as well as he did.

"It's okay," I said bravely, keeping my eyes firmly fixed on the scenery outside my window. Usually I hated all mention of my life before joining the Gypsies, but right now, oddly enough, I wanted to tell Sim so that he might know what it had been like. It was important that he understand.

"It used to be a kind of a game with Them," I said, meaning the other kids, the principal's daughter included. "They'd see just how far they could push me until I exploded. They got scared then and screamed for teacher, so guess who got in trouble? Then the minute the teacher's back was turned they'd be at it again, pushing and prodding. They just never quit." There was a bitter taste on my tongue.

"Those —!!" Sim spit the words out so savagely that my eyes flew to his face in alarm. He was watching the road with the intensity of a race-car driver.

I decided to change the subject. "Where are we going?" Some minutes ago I had noticed that Sim had smoothly skimmed by the turnoff to my block.

"Home," Sim said briefly, flashing me that smile of his. "My home this time. Come meet the parents and all that."

A little curl of something went through me—not exactly fear, not exactly nervousness—but some kind of ESP reaction. I made no protests about my job, saving them for a quick excuse home if something *did* happen.

"I suppose it's useless to ask what your house looks like?"

Sim kept grinning. "You got it, but guess away."

"Hmmm," I said, considering. "An igloo?" I asked lightheartedly, trying to repress any visions my mind might come up with to spoil the game. Sim was learning to accept my ESP, but only just, and I had no wish to ruin his surprise for me.

When we got within two miles of it he made me close my eyes. There was no difference in smoothness as we turned from the main road to the driveway, so I figured that it must be paved as well. My fingers tightened into fists. This was no igloo I was about to see.

What it was, was a mansion. No, I amended to myself, not a mansion—just a very large house on an acreage—make that a ten-acreage. The lawn stretched out till it hit a wooded thicket of poplars mixed in with evergreens.

"Hey!" Sim protested, "You peeked!"

I made no reply, fully occupied with just seeing as much as I could. *It would, after all, be the last time I saw it.*

I shivered suddenly, violently. Where had that thought came from? I was only fooling myself. I knew darn well where. I had to force myself to keep looking around, at the adorable gable windows, smart black trim and beautifully sculptured landscaping with large stones and dirt plots for flowers.

"I'm afraid it's not looking its best today. It's really something when the sun's out. Honest."

I looked at Sim in astonishment. How could he stand here amid all this beauty and apologize? Impulsively I took the two steps over to him and kissed him. "It's really something now." I wanted to thank him for showing it to me today, under all the dark clouds instead of in the bright sunlight as he probably loved it best.

Thunder rumbled low in the sky, and a strong wind sprang up, whipping my hair into Sim's face. I laughed low and joyously in my throat. There was nothing like a thunderstorm to put me in a good mood. And having Sim with me.

"Come on!" Sim grabbed my hand, and we both made a dash for the house.

The porch was big and clean, done in cool grays and blues. Not that I saw a lot of it. Sim pulled me almost immediately into the circle of his arms. "That kiss you gave me out there was way too short."

"True," I agreed, and we set about remedying it. Outside the storm broke in full force, rain driving down so hard the noise filled the room.

"What on earth—? Sim, is that you?" The voice came around the corner. Sim and I took a clumsy step apart. "Oh, my Lord!" The owner of the voice, a tall woman in a pink wool dress, took a firm grasp of the doorjamb to keep from falling.

"What is it, Mother?" Sim took a step towards her. "What's wrong?"

"Nothing's wrong," she denied sharply. "Not a thing. I heard the door slam and the automatic sprinkler go on, that's all." But she was lying. That wasn't what had made her cry out like that. It was me. For the first time in weeks, since Sim and I had started dating, I remembered my own looks, my out-and-out ugliness.

"Sprinkler?" I felt—rather than saw—Sim's frown. My eyes were locked with his mother's. Still an attractive woman, she had graying hair, though it must once have been as blond as Sim's.

"Yes, the sprinkler." She brushed this aside almost impatiently. "Don't tell me you didn't notice. The whole room is sopping wet."

In the electric silence which followed, both Sim and I looked at each other. We hadn't noticed a thing. Then we saw something far stranger: the only dry spot in the room was where we'd been standing. The automatic sprinkler had somehow managed to rain around us.

"Anyhow, Mother," Sim made an effort to shake off the tension that gripped us all, "this is Medusa. You told me to bring her down one of these days, and here she is!" His voice held an unmistakable note of pride.

"Yes, here she is," his mother agreed in that same flat tone that indicated shock. She had yet to drag her horrified eyes away from my face.

"Hello, Mrs. Trevellyan." I barely got the words past my throat. As always the mention of the name Trevellyan sent a wave of fierce anger through me.

"Hello, Medusa." My name seemed just as difficult for her to say, further heightening my anger. She seemed to get control of herself then, saying with effort, "Well, come on in. There's cake in the living room." She led the way, her spine held stiff and straight.

The inside of the house was just as showy as the outside. The living room was done in rich creams and browns. Even dessert matched, chocolate cake with white icing. The cake was good, I suppose. I deliberately kept a piece in hand as an excuse not to talk. Sim, perceptive as always, tried to keep the strain out of the conversation by telling his mother all sorts of funny things that happened at school. She did laugh, but only nervously, and her eyes kept flickering over to mine and then away again.

Why, I thought in amazement, she's afraid of me! And not just because of my face either—it's something else, something deeper. I frowned and tried to probe into her mind. It didn't work, of course. The Gift seldom did when forced. Instead my own anger began to increase by such leaps and bounds that I had to stop and concentrate hard on the brown velvet drapes, the only large dark area in the room.

Ostensibly, we were waiting for Sim's father to come home. When the phone rang Mrs. Trevellyan jumped a foot, practically running to answer it. There was a phone in the living room, a creamy white one with gold touches, so that she had to take it there in front of us.

"Hello, Dan? ... Yes, she's here." Her eyes slid across the room to rest on me. "Nooo ... Are you sure, Dan? There's no other way?" She bit down on her lip, and I thought I detected a bit of a sheen to her eyes. I looked away guiltily, feeling very much the eavesdropper.

"Well then, I suppose it can't be helped. Bye." Her disappointment showed in her reluctance to return the phone to its cradle and in her flat voice when she spoke to us. "That was your father, Sim. Something urgent has come up and he won't be able to make it until at least seven."

This was our exit cue, and Sim grabbed it with both hands. "It's time I took Medusa back."

I rose to my feet, murmuring thank-you's, gratefully following Sim's lead to the door. The brief shower outside was over though I had to pick my way through a few puddles to the pavement and Sim's car.

"Well, that went just great," Sim said grimly, letting the engine idle for a few minutes.

I somehow felt obligated to defend my actions. "I'm not used to talking to parents."

"I should say not!" Sim grinned suddenly. "Mother should be used to meeting my dates by now, even if she did find us kissing!"

I felt a brief prick of jealousy, quite strong, and praised God that I had nothing to be jealous of. The feeling was a new one to me, but it took only the example of my anger for me to know just how much stronger and more destructive an emotion it would be. That was the way it was with me; I had the power to hate with an intensity that was frightening.

Or to love.

That thought scared me, too. I quickly put a lid on that one. I had decided years ago that no one would ever be able to love me, ugly as I was, and with a temper apt to "erupt all over everything" in the words of one of my teachers, so it would be pure stupidity on my part to love somebody back.

And yet, the simple "See you tomorrow" parting from Sim, when he dropped me off at the Farmer's Market, had the power to wring my heart.

The next day didn't bring much of an opportunity to be alone with Sim, as Nancy Jean foisted herself on us at lunchtime. "Hi guys! Mind if I join you?" It was a rhetorical question since her tray was already on the table.

"Please, make yourself at home," Sim replied with thinly veiled sarcasm.

"Nice mood he's in today," Nancy Jean observed to me. "But never fear, I've brought just the thing to cheer him up. Ta dah!" she produced a magazine from behind her back.

Sim groaned and put a hand over his eyes. "What have I done to deserve this?" he appealed to the world in general.

We giggled as expected, and I asked, "What is it?"

"Well," a detectable gleam came into Nancy Jean's eye, "it's just a little magazine quiz."

"Hah!" scoffed Sim. "Don't believe a word of it! She's got out one of her horoscope things again."

"It is not!" she protested hotly. I smiled slightly watching first one's expression, then the other's.

"I'll believe that when I see it!" Sim crossed his arms with an air of finality.

We were beginning to attract more than our fair share of stares, so I ended the argument. "Well, if it isn't a horoscope, what is it?"

"It's a quiz, that's all." Nancy Jean sent Sim a "So there" look.

"Go on."

"Well," here she hesitated perceptively, "it does require that I know your birth dates."

Sim didn't pounce on this as I expected; he looked at me for some sign. I could see in his face that he was remembering what I had told him about my beginnings. I nodded slightly; my birth date was something they had been able to turn up at the hospital listed only under GIRL. The nurse on duty had remembered me (such an ugly little mite with crossed eyes and ears the size of Mr. Spock's.)

"Well, first of all, how old are you?"

Sim heaved a sigh. "Seventeen, as if you didn't already know." He took an enormous bite of his sandwich.

Nancy Jean ignored him and raised an eyebrow in my direction. "The same?"

"Seventeen," I confirmed, but I was no longer even looking in Nancy Jean's direction. I must have given the right advice about the sandwich this time; it was disappearing fast.

"Hey!" Nancy Jean snapped a finger under our noses, and said, not unkindly, "You can stare into each other's eyes another time, okay? Now then, please state your date of birth as accurately as possible."

"That's easy. I was the New Year's kid," Sim smiled mockingly, "born exactly one full second after midnight."

"Uh huh." Nancy Jean scribbled on her paper. "Medusa?"

My eyes hadn't left Sim's face, and I replied almost absently, "December 31st. One second before midnight." Sim had such blue, blue eyes....

"Are you sure?" Nancy Jean's excited voice burst in like a bombshell.

I frowned. "Yes. Unless of course the clock was a little off, but they're usually pretty good about that in hospitals, aren't they?"

"Weird," Nancy Jean breathed.

"What's weird?" Sim voiced the question I had been just about to ask.

Nancy Jean gave vent to a short, explosive sigh. "Neither of you two have been listening, have you? Why don't you tell each other what you just told me? When were you born, Sim?"

"On New Ye—"

"I heard the first time!" I interrupted angrily. "And I really don't see what—" But then I did see, and my impatience vanished to be replaced by a cold chill of what could only be fear.

"And Medusa was born on December the—" Nancy Jean prompted.

"Thirty-first." Sim let out a low whistle. "Within seconds of me."

"Providing both clocks were dead-on accurate," Nancy Jean pointed out. "A difference of two seconds isn't a lot."

From then on the conversation could very well have deteriorated to *Weird*'s and *they - always - said - truth - was - stranger - than - fiction*'s except for one little thing.

I saw him coming first, more with my ESP than my sight, and I grew quiet accordingly. It was Ralph, the bully who'd stood waiting outside the school the day Sim and I had gone to the cliffside. Other interested eyes were watching, waiting for the fun to begin, it seemed. No doubt they'd been the ones to egg him on in the first place.

His thoughts read like a laundry list, his sluggish mind having to plan in advance what he was going to say. He had flunked Grade 10 three times and the thing he wanted most in the world was a Honda scooter. He was a bully and a mean one, too, thinking his sheer size would overcome all who opposed him. Paint his face green and you'd have an admirable clone of the Incredible Hulk. Except the Hulk was smarter.

Only one point did I hold to: he hated Sim and everything he stood for. He wanted to hurt Sim. Bad. I was a girl. Sim's girl. He would first insult me and then get on to the business of breaking Sim into a dozen little pieces. Not here, of course. There were too many witnesses here to cry foul if he fought dirty or had several of his friends gang up on Sim. What he planned to do was issue a challenge like in all good Westerns: "High noon tomorrow. The alley. Be there."

There was only one flaw in his plan. He wasn't thinking in terms of what "a girl" would do.

I stood up to meet him. That threw him off guard for a couple of seconds, so he had to rethink his opening lines. A person less ruled by anger than myself would have brushed past him and avoided the whole thing, but I couldn't make myself. Oh no! That was too difficult. I was out of control already. And I completely forgot that, as far as everyone else was concerned, he hadn't done a thing yet. So I socked him good and hard.

I put all my strength behind the blow and, believe me, I rocked him. I took satisfaction in hearing the sickening crunch that went with a broken nose. A slow trickle of blood appeared out of his left nostril.

There were gasps around the room. One girl even screamed. Ralph looked justifiably stunned and more than a little pained. He put a hand up to his nose and seemed astonished when it came away with blood on it. "Why, you!" He started to come towards me.

I was still spitting mad and would have met him halfway, but Sim pushed me aside. I made no protest, feeling triumph pour through me. We stood together, united.

"Hello, Ralph." Sim's voice was deceptively mild, almost casual, but there was a glint to his eyes.

For a moment Ralph seemed confused, as he looked first from one to the other of us. His hand went again to his nose.

"Break it up! Break it up!" The Phys Ed teacher had an excellent pair of lungs, and he used them to good effect now, separating the two combatants. "Now what's this all about? Oh, it's you again." He surveyed Ralph with distaste.

"I didn't do nuthin'," Ralph protested, already shuffling backwards. "Ask anybody."

But the masses, when appealed to, kept their mouths shut, shifting their attention back to dinner.

"Uh huh," observed the Phys Ed teacher. "Well, to the school nurse with you anyhow." He quick-marched Ralph in front of him.

"You weren't kidding about breaking his nose, were you?" Sim said when at last we were sitting down again.

"No." So he did remember me asking Ralph's name. The thought oddly pleased me. In silence we both picked up our sandwiches.

"That's it?" The words, bursting from Nancy Jean as they did, came as something as a shock. I'd totally forgotten her, and from the look on Sim's face, I guessed he had as well. "That's all you're going to say?" she was incredulous.

"Well, yes," Sim said reasonably. "What else is there to say?"

"What else?" Nancy Jean was eyeing us as if we were both crazy. Especially me. "Besides the fact that you just broke some guy's nose for no good reason?"

Oh, but I did have a good reason, I told her silently. The best reason of all. Only she couldn't see that. Picking up her tray, she slammed her way out of the lunchroom. I looked after her with something akin to pity. "She doesn't understand," I remarked to Sim.

"Neither would I have, a month ago," Sim pointed out, and we both fell back to eating.

I stayed to watch badminton practice that day. I didn't usually, but then today was different. Nancy Jean's latest crush was on the team as well, and she and I sat together in the stands, earlier differences forgotten, cheering loudly when either of our players made a good hit. As we were the only two fans there, it was fairly obvious who Nancy Jean liked. After the game he wasted no time in asking her out for a soda.

She exchanged delighted looks with me and decided she didn't need a ride home after all. According to plan, I held Sim up an extra few minutes to allow them time to get a discreet distance ahead of us. Needless to say, everyone else was long gone.

Or at least they were supposed to be.

Ralph popped out from around a corner like the proverbial jack-in-the-box. "Hey, Trevellyan!" He now sported a large white bandage over his nose and even his smile looked greasy. He had Sim where he wanted him now. Within reach of his two fists and no teacher in sight.

"Something you wanted, Ralph?" Sim inquired, smiling widely, exposing a row of white even teeth. I was moved, ever so gently, to one side, and this time I stayed there. This was Sim's fight now, not mine.

"Yeah. I figure you owe me something." One huge hand went unconsciously up to his nose.

"Really, and what's that?" Sim was being extremely polite now, and for a moment Ralph frowned. Something was wrong here. Sim was smiling too much. Almost laughing. Yeah, that was it, Ralph said to himself. Sim was laughing at him.

"Why, you...!" And he took a swing.

Sim sidestepped neatly. "Why you what?" he asked mildly. The glint was back in his eye.

Ralph paused to think. His brows knotted. "Why, you!" And that was when Sim punched him. The fight didn't take long after that. A few solid hits by Sim, a few not-so-solid misses by Ralph, and the show was over.

Sim grinned at me and turned his back on Ralph. "Did I ever tell you I was a boxer in a past life?" He flexed one arm.

I started to answer, but the words died unspoken on my lips. Ralph was half-crouched on the floor behind Sim, fingering something shiny in his pocket. A knife—a thin, wickedly sharp switchblade! One foul, murderous thought gripped Ralph's mind as his muscles tensed to spring.

There was no time to scream, no time to fling myself in between the two of them—only time for a last anguished wail inside my head.

NOOOOOOOOOOOOOOOOOOOOOOOOOO!!!!!!!!!!!!!!!!

Ralph almost hesitated, swayed by the force of my will, but he didn't. And that was when the floor tilted. Ralph slipped sideways and a detention desk, normally pushed up against the side of the room, slammed into him. Hard. The air was driven out of his lungs in an audible Whoosh! The no-longer-stable earth shifted, lurched and rolled like a stormy sea. Knocked off balance, I stumbled forward, coming face to face with Ralph for one starey, sour-breath second before the next tremor threw me back.

Sim's arms caught me. "It's an earthquake," he shouted. "Take cover!"

Only there were no tables to cower under. Instead, Sim pulled me out of the way, hugging me against the wall. A great roaring filled my ears. Blindly, I turned my face into Sim's shirt to avoid the choking clouds of dust that rose around us.

When at last it was over, we stood there a moment longer, not trusting the suddenness of the reprieve. Neither Sim nor I had so much as a scratch on us.

There was a gaping hole in the roof over us, a dusty shaft of sunlight highlighting the pile of wreckage at our feet.

Sim took hold of the biggest piece and heaved. I helped, and a minute or two later when Nancy Jean came running back in, her date close on her heels, they joined us in pulling off board after board.

Under it all we found Ralph. Dead.

Chapter Seven

The Catalyst

I sat by myself on a lumpy couch hugging an equally lumpy pillow. I'd turned off all the lights around me, and the newscaster on TV was reflected a dozen times in all the windows.

Leo and Zsa and the others were out. A Gypsy celebration was in the making, complete with violin music and dancing. Originally, I had intended to go, but after one look at my face, Zsa had decreed that I stay home. No mention had been made of this afternoon's earthquake. So now here I sat going through my evening ritual of watching the ten o'clock news.

Not that garbage strikes and Lebanese terrorists particularly interested me, but an accurate weather report could go a long way in predicting tomorrow's mood for me. Yesterday's had said something about a low pressure system building up to the south with the threat of severe thunderstorms in the area. No mention of any other kind of disturbance.

But before the weather came the news.

"The earthquake that rocked the B.C. coast today, measuring 5.5 on the Richter Scale, was not so much unexpected as downright bizarre." The anchorman's plastic smile might have been hairsprayed in place for all its expression.

"Seismologists were shocked to find their instruments suddenly recording large L or earthquake waves. In the past an actual earthquake has always been preceded by several small tremors called P and S waves that signal to seismologists what is about to take place."

The TV maps called up vague memories of Grade 8 science lessons when we'd taken Earth Science. Funny, how I'd never thought of Lorelei as being on a fault line.

Standard pictures of rubble and wreckage began to flash on the screen. I stifled a yawn; today had been an exhausting day and I'd seen all this before anyhow. I might just as well head off to bed ... suddenly I sat up straighter. I had most certainly seen that place before, had passed it a multitude of times already on my way to and from school.

Sure enough the announcer's voice went on to say, "Damage was heaviest around the coastal town of Lorelei, B.C., seeming to get worse the closer you get to the heart of town. The epicentre, or exact origin of the quake, can be traced almost directly to this building."

Fear rose up and held me by the throat as the camera panned the letters "Lorelei High School." I knew with a sick certainty that I wanted to close my eyes and see no more. Only they wouldn't close, already one step ahead of the camera, now mounting the steps up to the school's heavy double doors.

I was in the hall again, helping to lift the last smashed desk that hid Ralph from view. As if everyone already knew he was dead, a sudden hush descended upon the rescuers, broken only by Nancy Jean's small choked cry as she turned blindly away from the sight and sobbed into someone's shoulder.

Sim had moved closer to me, saying with actions rather than words, that he was there if I needed someone to lean on. Only I didn't. All I could do was stand there, looking down at what was left of Ralph. I could feel no pity, only a kind of chill anger ... and perhaps that was most horrible of all. Ralph's hand was still in his pocket, the fingers clenched around his knife. He had meant to use it on Sim, and for that I was not ready to forgive.

I had hated him. If Sim had been harmed in any way I would have killed Ralph myself, and that was no exaggeration.

The weather came on next. With effort, I dragged my attention back to the ten-inch screen. I was getting pretty adept at reading the satellite maps myself and interpreted the curving lines to mean two fronts—one hot, one cold—were about to collide. Which meant basically that tomorrow could go either way.

The weatherman was getting quite excited, yabbering on about record highs and lows over the past 100 years, but I tuned him out, a cynical smile on my face. Weathermen were all alike. No matter where I'd travelled with the caravan, one of them was always raving about unusual weather patterns. *Either that or the bad weather purposely followed me around.*

I blinked suddenly, seriously considering for the first time the possibility that it was my bad moods that caused the weather, rather than the other way around. Cold began to creep into my bones, but I shrugged it off. I was being absurd, of course. Weathermen just acted that way naturally: it was the same with newsmen. Just look at the fuss they had made over the earthquake not having P and S waves. Or how they'd squawked about the "mysterious" power failure back in Winnipeg—

I swallowed hard, taking a sudden and rapid inventory of how many natural or man-made disasters I'd lived through. Besides the power failure, there was the orphanage fire when I was six; the mud slide of two years ago; today's earthquake, of course, and the chemistry class explosion one town back. There were too many. Far, far too many to have been mere coincidence.

And furthermore, the majority of them had happened when I was exceedingly angry for some reason or another.

So it was, after all, my fault. Every last bit of it, right down to Ralph's death this afternoon.

I had wanted him stopped and he had been stopped. Permanently.

The realization swept through my mind with the impact of a tornado, rapidly rearranging any previous conceptions I might have had about the earthquake and other disasters in the past. There was no surprise, only a kind of disbelief that I had not realized it before.

On the other hand, in a way, I had always known it. My thoughts flew back to when, as a young child, I had first made an effort to control my anger because Bad Things happened when I didn't. A little devil lived inside me, pounding against the walls of my mind, just waiting to be let out of its cage. Waiting. That was all. It needed nothing but time. For didn't I always, sooner or later, let it out of my own accord?

I came to, suddenly, my blunt fingernails embedded deep in the flesh of my palm. The TV was still on and I rose automatically, shutting up the newsman mid-sentence about a coming eclipse.

Outside, the violin music increased in tempo, the stomping of feet could be heard, and I felt more alone than usual.

Now that I thought about it, the earthquake was by no means an isolated incident. It was not even the first time someone had died.

The words Nancy Jean had quoted to Sim in the car sprang to mind, "All kinds of weird things happen around this object, but the object itself remains unchanged."

That was what I was. A Catalyst. Harming all that wandered into my path. No bloody wonder I'd been abandoned.

Oh, the orphanage had tried to soften the exact wording, but the story of my finding had really been too spectacular to keep from being retold again and again.

It was two in the morning when the call came through. Someone in town had seen a brief flare about twenty miles down the highway, and they were wondering if it might've been an accident. So, dubiously, the police set out.

No other lights had been seen, and they were almost ready to turn back. The driver had in fact slowed, looking for a place to turn around and that was what saved me. And possibly them as well.

The highway had a slight dip to it, a blind spot in one place. If it hadn't been for the fresh skid marks, the police might well have done as the other car had done. Come up over the hill a shade too fast, seen the outline of a child framed by the headlights, swerved violently, and missed me only by inches before going over the bank.

Both of the people in the car had died, and I had been taken, smiling, to the orphanage. No one could ever explain how I came to be on that road in the first place, and I was too young to be of any help—a toddler with a ten-word vocabulary.

I had been "lucky, incredibly lucky," and I'd been told so repeatedly, in between speeches based on the theme "Don't make trouble." Until now, those very words were as a spark to kindling. I'd told Russell there was "No such thing as luck," and I'd meant it. Most things, I'd found out, had both a purpose and a cause.

The root of all the "happenings" around me was my anger. No, I frowned suddenly, that wasn't quite true. My feelings had nowhere even approached anger the night Sim's car went on the blink, or when the sprinkler system had gone off over our heads. Fights broke out around me in school with frightening regularity. All that was required was that I be there.

My years at the orphanage were sheer misery, my memories of it always tinged with grayness—neither black nor white. Rarely a day went by without the Anger coming over me. There were so many things to be angry at. The frustration of trying to do schoolwork I couldn't understand; the other children poking fun at me, or being shunned by them altogether; the not-quite-hidden revulsion in the teachers' eyes when they looked at me; even the girl in the bed beside mine who'd always insist on having a night light and who cried to the matron when I unplugged it.

I had no friends. All the other children either hated me or were scared of me. With reason. I was too ugly to be adopted, and the two foster families I'd been sent out to hadn't worked either. Were there any place to go to, I would have run away. The advent of Madame Rosa when I was thirteen had been the answer to a prayer.

The caravan had travelled many months to find me, stopping often along the way. Until Madame Rosa had the Death dream there was no hurry. She knew she was dying, of course. Had her psychic ability not told her, the deterioration of her health would have. Madame Rosa both knew and accepted it, but she could not die without first choosing her successor. Me.

None of the others in the caravan had any talent anywhere near her's, Zsa coming in a faint second. The crystal had been Madame Rosa's specialty, and she had used it to lead the caravan unerringly to the doorstep of the orphanage. She had known me on sight, though unable to describe me beforehand—much to the matron's dismay when Zsa and Leo came knocking.

The officials at the orphanage did not trust the Gypsies, claiming a caravan to be an "unsuitable home," but in the end they were just as happy to be rid of me as I was them.

Zsa and Leo took me immediately to the caravan and to an old woman confined to her bed. Madame Rosa did not flinch when she saw my face. Instead, she took both my hands in her wrinkled ones for a reading. "You are of Gypsy blood," she pronounced carefully, eyes holding mine. "The Gift is strong in you and this is good. You will need it."

Then she began to speak in Romanee, her voice rising and falling in natural cadences, so that the English words, when she uttered them, were that much harsher. Her brown eyes blurred, looking through me to something beyond. "Unto the seventh generation it will follow."

She fell back on the pillows and the light faded from her eyes, her clawlike hands still gripping the bed covers. Zsa detached herself from the background, gently leading me away. "She is dead. She had foreseen it and so it has happened. You are her chosen successor. You are one of us now."

Life on the road had come easily to me. Being one step ahead of whomever was after us added the spice of danger. The Gypsy culture, rich in costumes and traditions dating back to pre-Christian times, fascinated me. I picked up Romanee as if I'd been born to it. Released from the orphanage, I'd revelled in my freedom. I'd always had an itch to travel, and there was never anything I couldn't bear to leave behind.

School had not gotten easier although my classmates were more subtle in their digs and needling. The knockdown fights of the elementary grades were a thing of the past—with rare exceptions, of course—so in junior high I discovered the fine art of self-preservation.

I learned to blend into the background, generating as little interest as possible and living on the fringes of student life. I wanted to be left to myself and so I was. I sat at the back of every class, looking forward only, playing dumb when I was called on to answer a question, and studying only enough to pass. I never spoke unless spoken to, and not always then either. Days went by when all I did at school was shrug. Had it not been a matter of pride in the form of one girl sneering that I "would never finish school anyhow, so why didn't I just give up?" I would have quit school altogether.

And out of school, there was the fortuneteller's tent. At first Zsa had much to teach me in the ancient art of palmistry—the reading of lines and mounds—and the meanings of the major and minor arcana of the tarot deck. Soon though, I surpassed her, practising for hours and refining my Gift. As it was my only talent, I would have been a fool to let it go to waste.

The Catalyst thing I had singlemindedly ignored; reviewing the evidence, I could see that now. Only a blind man could have missed the clues. I only had to walk by for the pop machine to malfunction and spurt out fizzy pop, or the telephone to ring, or the film projector to tangle the reels. Anything mechanical was meat. Others had noticed, earning me the nickname "Battery Killer" back in Clapton, but still I had managed to ignore what was right in front of my nose.

There would be no more of that, I vowed. But what to do? I was a menace to society. A town back down the line, the discovery would have made no difference. Zsa and Leo were really the only ones who came in contact with me; and they, I suspected, knew the risks better than I did. Madame Rosa must have warned them. Except here in Lorelei there were others to consider. Nancy Jean and Sim.

What was I going to do? Three possible solutions presented themselves, none of which I liked. Letting the whole thing slide would be a mistake—I *knew* that. I could tell my friends everything and leave the decision up to them, or simply skip out of town entirely. The last solution would be the fairest to them, for I had a pretty shrewd idea that neither Sim nor Nancy Jean would desert me, and I had ties with them as well. When it came down to the nitty gritty I was not sure that I could leave Sim without a word of good-bye. I had a feeling he might come after me, and he'd find me, too. I did a slow burn remembering his words, "I always know where you are."

I picked up my deck of tarot cards, shuffled them seven times, and dealt myself a three-card spread, each card signifying my past, present and future.

Death came up first. That was easy enough to interpret with Ralph not yet in his grave.

The other two cards were also of the major arcana—no Cups, Wands, Swords or Pentacles here. Powerful forces were at work.

The next card, The Tower, represented my present and was hardly more encouraging. It depicted a stone tower struck by lightning and two people in the act of falling from its heights. Sim and I? I wondered uneasily. The Tower spoke of ruin, danger and unforeseen disaster. To a lesser extent, it represented courage, something I felt sure I would need.

The future had no less powerful a card in The Hanged Man. Although not as gruesome as it sounded—the man was suspended by his feet, not his neck—the card still spoke of martyrdom and sacrifice. I searched my mind desperately for any good connotations the card might bring but could only think of one: the vague promise of regeneration and transition to a new life.

All in all, not a terribly helpful reading. In the end I went to bed and slept on it, only to awaken no nearer an answer than before.

Only the junior high section of the school had sustained serious damage. For the rest of us, it was business as usual. I purposely got there late, ostensibly to avoid any camera crews that might still be hanging around, but really because I didn't feel up to facing Nancy Jean or Sim. I slipped into class just as the bell rang, resolutely avoiding Nancy Jean's questioning look. Mr. Farr started class so that she had no choice but to open her book and take up the questions.

The either-way forecast had swung in sunshine's favour. By question number four I was beginning to feel distinctly woozy. Spots of light danced before my eyes and the pressure on my temples became a measurable thing. I had to shut my eyes, finding blessed relief in the darkness.

"Medusa!" Mr. Farr's voice ripped through my mind like a grappling hook. My hands flew to my ears, and I cradled a head suddenly racked with pain.

"Wakey-wakey! You're not in playschool anymore." Mr. Farr was furious, radiating hostile vibrations as he stomped down the aisle to my desk. "We no longer have naptime!"

A familiar warning chill raised the hairs on my neck. The monster in me had found the key to its cell. *Go away!* I screamed at Mr. Farr silently. *Don't you know any better than to take the lid off Pandora's box?*

"Wake up, I say!"

I opened my eyes, closing them again instinctively. The light hurt them badly, sending pinpricks of pain out all over my body. My tongue had long ago cleaved to the roof of my mouth, and had I been able to speak I would have demanded fiercely, "Satisfied? Are you satisfied now?"

But of course he wasn't. He kept on yelling, each word a bludgeon at my skull. "I don't care how many late-night parties you've been out to. Nobody goes to sleep in my class!"

Late-night parties. That was so far from the truth it was almost funny. Almost.

"Nobody, do you hear me?"

I heard him. Anger poured into me, roaring through my veins at such a rate that only in the far, far off background did I hear Nancy Jean telling him to shut up and couldn't he see I was ill.

Oh yes, I laughed hysterically to myself. *I'm ill. I've got a terminal case of temper.* The anger swelled far past the point where I usually let it out of the bottle. I began to shake from the sheer effort of suppressing it. I was on a roller coaster ride now, and once on, there was no getting off until the ride was over. For a moment I teetered precariously on the brink and then began the long, swift journey down.

At that moment the lights began to go out in the classroom, one by single one. My field of vision narrowed, focused like a telescope, and vanished into blackness. In the tradition of fortunetellers and mediums, I was going into a trance.

✣✣✣✣✣✣✣✣✣✣✣✣✣✣✣✣✣✣✣✣✣✣✣✣✣✣✣✣✣✣✣✣✣✣✣✣✣✣✣

it was of the future,
mine and sim's future
where the light and the dark overlapped
for a time
and then—
sim was DYING and it was my fault
MY fault my FAULT MY fault my FAULT MY fault
and i must do something but what can i do?

i can sense words

but i know not what they mean

there is TREVELLYAN

and there is

hatred

TREVELLYAN did this, TREVELLYAN

must

pay

unto the first generation

unto the second generation

unto the third generation

unto the fourth generation

unto the fifth generation

unto the sixth generation

Unto the Seventh Generation

✣✣✣✣✣✣✣✣✣✣✣✣✣✣✣✣✣✣✣✣✣✣✣✣✣✣✣✣✣✣✣✣✣✣✣✣✣

When I came to, I was sprawled across a chair in what I took to be the principal's office. My eyes, after the first flutter, remained instinctively closed. I was in desperate need of darkness.

Sim was on one side of me, supporting me and holding my hand. I knew that without even having to open my eyes—in no other's arms could I have relaxed so completely. I stirred slightly and Sim "shhhhed" me. For a few precious minutes I let myself stay there before opening my eyes and straightening.

"Was it bad?" Sim's tone was soft and understanding. I felt immediately that he *knew.* He had the Gift as well, if Gift it could be called.

The stark black-and-white images of the trance flashed through my mind for the space of a second, and I broke out in gooseflesh, only able to nod. It had been very bad.

Silence, a living golden thing in itself, filled the room.

Of course it couldn't last. From the hall came raised angry voices, one of them Mr. Farr's. More fighting. A Catalyst's work is never done.

"I tell you, the girl was being deliberately obtuse. Why, I wouldn't put it past her to have just pretended to faint!" And so on.

My head began to thud again. All I'd ever wanted was to be left alone. Was that such a monstrous thing to ask?

"Yes, yes, it is." Sim's vehemence was totally unexpected, and I turned shocked eyes in his direction. "Nobody should have to be alone."

I continued to stare at him. He'd heard what I was thinking and he didn't even seem to realize it was out of the ordinary! I opened my mouth to speak, but someone else stole the march on me.

"What, Trevellyan? You here?" It was the principal, a little taken aback at finding us in *his* office. "Shouldn't you be in class?" he lightly scolded. Sim, I noticed, had a habit of making friends in high places as well as low.

"Yes sir, I suppose I should be." Sim was, as always, respectfully polite. "I just came to check up on Medusa here."

"I trust you're feeling better, uh, Medusa?" For the first time he seemed to notice my presence.

The hackles rose on the back of my neck, but I managed to remain civil. "Yes."

"Well, then...." He made a vague, dismissing gesture towards the door and bent over some papers.

My feet had taken on that rooted feeling again. Sim nearly had to drag me out the door. "Come on. We need to talk."

I agreed wholeheartedly. The halls were deserted, and I took a deep breath ready to tell him about the Catalyst business. Only Fate did not want me to spill my guts just yet.

"Psst!" The sound and a beckoning hand came from around the next corner. "Come here, but be quiet!"

We came. It was Nancy Jean, who snaked out a hand and yanked us unceremoniously around the corner and out of sight. Her eyes were as big as dinner plates and her cheeks pink from excitement. "What's going on? Are you going home now, Medusa? You're still pale. I tried to keep that dumb Mr. Farr from yelling at you, bu—"

Sim smoothly interrupted her flow of words. "Why aren't you in class?"

Nancy Jean brushed that aside with a toss of her head. "I skipped out, of course. Where've you been, Sim? I've been peeking in all the windows trying to find you to tell you about Medusa."

Sim's eyes found mine, and I read in them a repetition of his words on the cliff: *I always know where you are.*

"Well, I guess you've already found her on your own," observed Nancy Jean. "Did you just come out of the principal's office? Was he mad? Or ... ?"

"Yes to the first and no to the second." Sim kept his patience, even smiling a little. "Now I have a question of my own. Why is Mr. Farr so upset? I had him a couple of years back, and he seemed like an okay guy then."

"He usually is," agreed Nancy Jean, "but something about Medusa just seems to rub him the wrong way."

I spoke for the first time then, bitterly, "I have that effect on a lot of people. You see," here I took a deep breath ... there was really no easy way to say it and now was as good a time as any, "I'm what your friend Russell calls a Catalyst. I make things happen."

Nancy Jean looked anxiously at Sim as if to say, "She's sicker than I thought," and she reached over to pat my shoulder.

I threw off her hand, practically yelling, "I am not sick!"

Nancy Jean looked startled. Too late, I remembered that the words hadn't actually been said outloud. Well, too late now. I plunged on, "I am a Catalyst. I'm cursed."

"Of course you're not," Nancy Jean's tone was soothing. Her eyes didn't move from mine as she slowly began to draw near. "You're overwrought, that's all. What you need is a good, strong cup of—"

I wanted to scream at her. Overwrought? I was furious! She didn't believe me. Didn't want to believe me. Ah, there lay the sore point. "Shut up!" I snapped.

Nancy Jean looked at me as if I'd gone mildly insane, and at the moment I wasn't far from it. "Don't you see?" I was practically stamping my foot with impatience now. "I'm the one who caused the earthquake! I'm the one who killed Ralph!"

I saw the fear leap into her eyes, and I responded to it, lashing out against myself as much as them. "If you've got half a brain in your head, you'll run like the dickens and never come back! Both of you." I turned to Sim as well, rejecting but unable to keep that last bit of pleading out of my eyes.

"Then I guess I only have half a brain." Sim moved up quietly and put an arm around my shoulders. He didn't have to say anything more—the look on his face read plainer than words. I felt enormous relief. The curse didn't make a bit of difference to him. Not one bit.

When I spoke to Nancy Jean again, I was calmer, kinder almost. "Think about it. Just think about it. Remember the day you joined me in the cafeteria and you got so mad? I did that."

"Of course you did," Nancy Jean was still searching for excuses. "I was mad at you."

I tried again. "And the night of the Valentine's Day Dance? Who do you think made the speaker whine, and the balloons pop?"

"That was just a unfortunate coincidence." This time she sounded just the tiniest bit uncertain.

"There are no such things as coincidences," I spoke positively, convincingly. "There was a storm that night and for two days after it. I did that, as well as all the power failures at school. I affect everything around me." I had a sudden stroke of inspiration. "I've affected you. Think about it. You've gone through an awful lot of boyfriends in the past month. How close was I sitting each time you broke up?" I knew I'd hit a nerve the moment I said it. Nancy Jean's face crumpled.

Sim chuckled suddenly. I looked at him quizzically; I didn't see anything to laugh about.

"I just thought of something," he explained. "You're probably the one to thank for the breakdown at the Galaxy Arcade. The machine wouldn't take my quarters."

"I try my best," I said modestly. Now that Sim mentioned it I could remember the occasion quite well. I'd liked the darkness of the Arcade and had wanted to stay.

"And all the cafeteria food fights, that was you?" Nancy Jean's head came up now, and she looked at me with something akin to awe.

I grinned suddenly. "Well, maybe not all of them."

"Whoa!" Nancy Jean speechless was quite the sight to see. In the end she tried to make a joke out of it. "Good thing you don't take Chemistry." I could feel my face freeze, but Nancy Jean rushed on heedlessly. "Can you imagine the explosion?"

"As a matter of fact I can," I told her in a strained voice. "I was in one last November."

Now it was Sim's turn to look like he'd been hit with a load of bricks. "So was I."

Chapter Eight

Two of a Kind

Nancy Jean looked first from one to the other of our white faces. "Look, you two need some place quiet to talk." She glanced at her watch. "It's nearly lunch. In a couple of minutes this place will be crawling with students. How about coming to my house to eat? My parents won't mind if I have a couple of friends over."

"Okay," Sim agreed immediately. I raised no objections, allowing myself to be trundled off to Sim's red machine. We did need to talk. My mind was still reeling from the implications of Sim being there when the Chem lab blew sky high. And where else was there to go? Certainly not to the caravan and just as certainly, not to Sim's house. I was never going to see it again, remember?

Nancy Jean's house was in town, a large rambling affair. The yard boasted a tree house and a fort as well as several sizes of rusty bikes and a skateboard. I'd been astounded the first time I saw her place until Nancy Jean explained to me that she was one of a family of eight with three younger and two older brothers and sisters. The house was comfortably messy, but clean.

It was also, for the moment, completely empty of people. The note on the kitchen table told all. Suzy had had a toothache, and her mother had taken her into Clapton to see the dentist. All the other kids were in school, and her dad took lunch on the job.

We munched on crackers in the living room and began to untangle the mess facing us, starting with this morning's escapade. I knew relatively little, having blacked out so soon into the argument. Mr. Farr, Nancy Jean said, had kept right on yelling even though I'd keeled over practically onto the floor. She'd gotten through to him in the end that something was wrong, but once I'd been established in the office she'd been unceremoniously shipped back off to class.

I let Nancy Jean fill us in, adding only, "I had a headache. A bad one. And when I get them my mind seems to stop functioning." I made no mention of my trance. It upset me too much to talk about, and besides, Nancy Jean wouldn't understand. How could she?

"Oh, hang on," Nancy Jean jumped up. "There's something I've been meaning to show you for a while." She ducked out of the room leaving me and Sim alone. His eyes, when they met mine, were questioning. He knew I'd had a trance.

The little prickle of gooseflesh that oftentimes comes with an ESP flash, crawled up my spine. "Something is going to happen," I spoke involuntarily. "Something bad ... that has to do with you and me and ... something else. Someone else,"

I corrected myself, frowning. "There is a connection," I thought aloud. "There has to be one, if only we could find it."

"Then we will find it," Sim said with certainty, and he imposed a time limit. "Soon."

I felt a kind of panicky sensation in my throat. Yes it must be soon, before it was too late to stop this—this THING. If indeed it was possible to stop.

The Chem lab seemed the logical place to start, and so we began, filling in the missing pieces for each other.

Sim started, "It was my second day in the building, my first day of classes."

I chewed on my lip, considering. That would explain why I'd never see him around Clapton, but not how we'd missed seeing one another within the small confines of one Chemistry lab.

"Dad was reorganizing an office there, and rather than wait at home Mother and I went with him. On location, so to speak. I got directions to the class and joined it about halfway through. I hadn't done much more than find myself a place to sit down when Foom! There was this tremendous explosion."

"I know," I said quietly, the picture of the girl's bleeding face flashed through my mind. She had hated me on sight. "I was in the closet, you see, and when I stepped out ... Boom!" I gave a creditable imitation of Sim's sound effects.

"In the closet? What on earth were you doing in there?" Sim leaned forward, blue eyes intent.

"Hiding," I said baldly and had the momentary satisfaction of knowing I'd surprised him.

"From what?"

My mouth twisted. "Don't you know? It's quite obvious once you think about it." He couldn't have watched me for so long without noticing how I always chose the deepest shadow and flinched away from what he loved.

"The light." Sim's voice sounded heavy.

"Yes, the light," I agreed.

A silence fell between us, broken wide open by Nancy Jean's voice. "Aren't you forgetting something here?"

Sim jumped, and I turned lazily to look in the direction of her voice. I hadn't consciously noted her return, but my ESP must have picked up on it because I wasn't in the least surprised. "And what's that?"

"What brought you together in the first place. The Unlikely Coupleship." Nancy Jean was bubbling over with excitement.

"Yes?" Sim and I turned two identically blank faces to hers.

She rolled her eyes. "Look, we didn't just pick your two names out of a hat, you know. You both filled in the forms which were then fed into the computer, and the computer did the match-ups."

"So?" I prompted her again.

"So, the highest match for the ten Most Likely couples was eighty-two percent. Your score was zero. You disagreed on *everything!*"

Sim and I exchanged looks. "Uh huh," I offered helpfully.

Nancy Jean gave a snort of disgust. "Really! How can two people be so dense?"

"It might help," Sim suggested mildly, "if you cut out the theatrics and got to the point."

For an answer Nancy Jean got up and shoved two papers into our unwilling hands. "I snitched these out of the Students' Union office. They were so weird I just had to keep them. Take a look, and then tell me you don't know what I mean!"

I had an uneasy flashback to Mrs. Hopkins glaring at me in much the same way over my one-hundred-percent C.I.Q. score. This paper, however, had no line of red check marks. I looked up questioningly.

Nancy Jean sighed. "Question One," she read, "What kind of colouring do you have? Sim?"

"Fair."

"Medusa?" She raised an inquiring eyebrow in my direction.

"Dark," I read off my sheet. It was rather symbolic, but surely there was nothing remarkable about that? Ditto to question two which dealt with height.

"Personality type?"

"Fun-loving," Sim rattled off his answer and sagged back into the couch.

I responded in kind, "Intense," but a small shiver crept up my spine. I was beginning to see what Nancy Jean had been getting at.

Looks was the next category, and Sim shifted uncomfortably on the couch, catching my eye almost apologetically. "I filled in handsome. There were a bunch of us doing them at the same time, and it seemed ... funny," he explained needlessly.

"Ugly," I said in a flat tone of voice. I had not been joking.

The questions went on, all twenty-five of them, and the only ones that did not seem to be in exact conflict was the favourite colour. Sim's was yellow, and mine was, of course, black.

The atmosphere was distinctly weird by now, and I really didn't need Nancy Jean to pipe up and remind us that, "Yellow is the colour that shows up best on black."

And that was only the beginning.

Using the incredible coincidence of our birth dates as a starting point, I described my tragic circumstances of being found as an orphan on the road. "I killed them. I'm responsible." My mind was suddenly plagued with images of a car swerving off the road, and the images were not wholly imagined. I could clearly see the face of the young woman driving, see the force with which her head hit the dash.

"Medusa!" Sim shook my shoulder. "Medusa, look at me!"

I turned my head blearily in his direction, the woman in my vision superimposed over his face. How red the blood seemed against the pallor of her skin. She had died instantaneously.

"It wasn't your fault, Medusa! It wasn't!"

"No?" I said bitterly, snapping out of it. "Then whose fault was it?"

"Not yours," Sim was adamant. "Never yours." He said the words softly, almost reverently, his eyes never leaving my face. For a moment I felt as close to beautiful as I was ever likely to get.

Nancy Jean cleared her throat noisily, startling the both of us. "Tell me about the orphanage."

"I was an outcast," I said, talking for the first time without bitterness or self-mockery. "The rest of the kids hated me, and I wasn't too ... friendly ... towards them. The matrons didn't know what to do with me. My Second Sight unnerved them, and my temper frightened them. Sometimes I almost frighten myself," I added softly. "When the Gypsies appeared, I leapt at the chance to go with them. It was either that or run away."

Sim smiled, and when I looked at him sharply he apologized, "Sorry, it just sounded so ... melodramatic. Like how they do it in the movies. Girl Runs Away to Join Circus," he read an imaginary newspaper headline.

"I am of Gypsy blood," I said simply. "I wanted to travel. The orphanage was killing me in more ways than one."

Sim's eyes looked suddenly haunted. "How can you say that?" he demanded passionately. "How can anybody like being constantly on the move, always leaving things and people behind, never knowing where you might find yourself next?"

Nancy Jean and I looked at him in astonishment. What had brought this on?

"I hate travelling," Sim said unnecessarily. "Until I was thirteen that was virtually all we did, move from one town to another. The last place was this horrid little dump in the backwaters of New Brunswick. That's when Mother put her foot down and we got the house here in Lorelei. Clapton was only for a few months, nothing more."

I took a sudden, sharp breath; the air like a knife in my lungs. "Would you—would you happen to remember the name of the town?"

Sim gave a mock shudder. "As if I could ever forget. It was called Bliss, and a more joyless place I've never seen."

I cringed. "Joyless and as dull as dishwater." Sim looked at me in surprise and I explained. "I lived in the Bliss County Home for the Homeless. I left when I was thirteen, too."

After that, the parallels came thick and fast. It was more than spooky. It was downright frightening. Sim struggled to put it into words. "It's like we're two of a kind. Only opposites. There's some kind of bond between us. Some link that's beyond our control."

And there Sim hit the nail squarely on the head. Through it all, and all the time we were talking I had this curious feeling of destiny. Of things beyond my control. It was a helpless feeling, and I didn't care for it one bit. It made all our present discoveries futile and mocked our efforts to understand. Something was going to happen, something that had waited a long time for its chance, and it wasn't going to be thwarted by mere humans.

Another fragment of my trance came back to me. "Unto the seventh generation." It sounded almost biblical. I put the question to Sim, but he just shrugged. I raised my voice slightly, "Nancy Jean?"

A light frown creased her forehead. "I don't really know. Maybe something about the sins of the father being visited onto his children? Oh!" She suddenly sat bolt upright. "I just thought of something. Be right back." So saying, she vanished back into the kitchen. She was back within seconds to inquire, "What are your full names? Middle ones included."

"Simson Benedict Perseus Trevellyan," Sim grimaced. "Quite the mouthful, isn't it?"

"Pretty bad," I agreed. "But I can top it. Medusa Jobyna Leila plus whatever last name you care to tack on."

"Thanks." And she was gone again. I smiled, sitting still was a real chore for her; I was surprised she'd lasted this long.

"You never did tell me," Sim began, "how you knew my name."

"I read it on your palm," I said, no more evasions this time. There was a need to know on both sides. "Don't forget I'm a card-carrying psychic. I've been making a living out of this for years."

Sim looked relieved. "And your reaction? More theatre?"

I hesitated, sensing how much Sim wanted me to say yes, but too much had been lied about already. "No. That surprised me just as much as it surprised you." I paused for a moment and admitted flatly, "I hate your last name." Even now I could not bring myself to say the word. Trevellyan. My eyes narrowed and lips curled up.

"And me?" The question came out softly, almost tentatively.

I smiled genuinely. "No, not you." It was on the tip of my tongue to say "I love you," but I pulled back just in time. For one heart-stopping second I thought Sim had read it in my face, and I tensed.

Like a draft of fresh air Nancy Jean burst into the room, wildly waving a book and almost hitting Sim in the nose. "Guess what I found! It's so absolutely, positively weird! I mean, I thought the computer forms were bad enough, but this is fantastic!"

Nancy Jean's excitement was infectious, but I felt more than a few twinges of apprehension as well. Sim's fingers met and laced with mine. For once he made no joking comments, allowing Nancy Jean to tell of her discovery in her own confused and jumpfrogging way.

"It's what I was telling you about the opposites. Total opposites. I mean, one set of names would be strange, but three sets is incredible!" Nancy Jean was practically overflowing with words, but somehow I was having a hard time making sense out of what she was saying. Sim looked as bewildered as I felt. She took pity on us and slowed down enough to show us what she meant. "Here!" The book came out again, and she tapped a specific spot, barely allowing me to glimpse my name before flipping along to the next spot. "And here!" Her hoop earrings swung out as she turned her head.

Sim took her hand. "Please Nancy, wouldn't it be easier to just tell us?"

Nancy Jean slowed herself down with effort and began to enunciate clearly. "You were talking about generations, and it suddenly occurred to me that we'd given little thought to that side of the story. I mean, the one connection that we do have with your past," she nodded at me, "is the name. You said your Mother wrote it out on some kind of name tag. Why? What possible reason could she have had for doing it? So I checked out the meanings. On both of your names."

Nancy Jean had a look on her face similar to that of a small child loosed in a candy store. "And they matched!"

I looked down now at the page in the name book that Nancy Jean had been trying to show us and then looked up again. "You tell us."

My calmness reassured her, and she grinned. "Actually they didn't have Medusa in the book, so I looked it up under Greek mythology. She was a Gorgon, one of those creatures who could turn people to stone with a look and had snakes for hair. That sort of thing. Anyhow," Nancy Jean dragged herself back on track. "She was slain by a handsome Greek warrior by the name of Perseus."

There was a moment of electric silence, and Sim's hand tightened convulsively on mine. Nancy Jean was tactful enough not to point out the similarities of the present situation with the Gorgon's ugliness and the Greek warrior's good looks, but that didn't mean that either of us were unaware of them.

"I looked up Jobyna next. It means the accursed, and Benedict means the blessed."

Of course, I thought with that rational calm, how very appropriate.

"Your third name, Leila, means darkness." Nancy Jean studied us both carefully before dropping the last of her bombshells. "And Simson means sunlike."

Light and dark. The two contrasts of nature.

I remembered fleetingly how, when Sim chased me after the dance and demanded to know who I was, I had replied, quite easily and naturally that I was Darkness.

And then I thought of my Mother whom I couldn't remember and who had chosen my three names, taking time to pin them to me in the form of a name tag so that they would stay with me all my life. Did she have the Gift as I do, and know how true the meanings would ring? Was this her way of reaching from beyond the grave to somehow warn me?

And then I thought of Sim's mother, whom I had seen, and of the horrified recognition in her eyes when she'd looked at me. She too had played a part in the naming, but I somehow could not credit her with such an exact matching of names. I would have been the last person she would have cared to link in any way with her child.

The same chill came creeping into my blood as I met Sim's eyes over the coffee table. He answered my unspoken question. "My Dad named me."

What on earth could it all mean?

Chapter Nine

The Total Eclipse of the Heart

Of course I knew about the eclipse.

It had only been on everyone's lips for months—the one topic of conversation that never failed, even after that of the weird weather was exhausted.

The little tiny dot of a town, Lorelei, was going to experience a total solar eclipse. The moon would cross in front of the sun, and for the space of a few minutes we would lie in the moon's darkest shadow. More importantly, though the thought did not cross my mind at the time, there would be night during the day.

Television and radio alike were filled with warnings not to look at the sun during the eclipse because the part still showing would do permanent damage to the retina of the eye. Sim even went so far as to make me promise not to even peek while it went on. To him, sight was the most precious gift of all and a lifetime spent in the dark of blindness would be a veritable nightmare. My concern was not so great, but I promised all the same. "Why look at the moon when you have twenty little moons already?" he said smiling.

"No, I don't."

Sim looked momentarily startled. "Of course you do. On your fingernails and toenails. Everyone has them."

"I don't," I stated cheerfully, letting Sim examine my hands for himself. There were no little crescent moons at the base of each fingernail. Not even small ones. He just shook his head.

Classes were scheduled as usual for the day of the eclipse. Everyone was expected to watch the live broadcast of the eclipse on one of the several networks who had TV crews on location in the area. It promised to be a major event. Heaven knows by the time it was over everyone would have had their fill and more.

The sense of something in the wind affected everyone that day. Classes were rowdier than usual, with much jostling, not all of it friendly. Even the teachers seemed restless, but for me it was worse. I was literally walking on a knife's edge.

I also had the makings of a migraine, but it was more than that: I felt all wound up inside. I had an awful premonition that before the day was out Something was Going to Happen. On the way to school this morning, the feeling of eyes on my back hadn't helped any, and I'd all but growled at the poor kid behind me. He had slipped on the ice immediately afterward. Chalk up one for the Catalyst. Mr. Farr's precious adding machines were already acting up, and I knew that it wouldn't take much more than a nudge to push me over the edge. I waited until Mr. Farr's back was turned before slipping out the door.

Sim was waiting for me in the hall. For him I dredged up a smile.

I had long ago stopped asking how he knew exactly when things would get to be too much for me. I didn't particularly care.

He too seemed in a state of nervous excitement, ducking around a corner with me when we heard a teacher approaching. Only it wasn't a teacher—teachers didn't softfoot it down their own hallways—it was Russell. I held my breath as he passed by, consulted the map in his hand, and knocked on the Accounting Room door.

As quiet as ghosts, Sim and I turned and vanished down the hallway, but not before Russell began to speak.

He was asking about me.

The realization came with a jolt; there was almost an audible click as I connected him with the feeling of being watched this morning. No room for doubt there. The anger rose within me so that I came close to going back and blacking his eye—I felt extremely violent today—but Sim caught the look and hustled me down the hallway and out of doors.

We were well into March now, and it was warm enough that jackets were no longer needed. Sim stretched tall, basking in the sun. "Those fluorescent lights inside just aren't the same."

The light bombarded me from all directions, and I swayed dizzily, clutching for but not finding the rail. "Sim!"

He turned, quick as a cat, and caught me, pulling me safely back into the shadows. I leaned gratefully back against the cool stone of the wall, eyes closed.

"Sorry, I wasn't thinking. You gonna be okay?" Sim squatted down to my eye level.

"I'll be fine." Painfully I dragged my eyelids back up over my eyes only to shut them again. Ouch! The next time I was more cautious, squinting through my eyelashes. The pounding in my head began anew; it even hurt to think. I had a sudden mental picture of Russell striding purposely down the hallway towards the doors. Right now. He was looking for me, and I had no intention of letting him find me. "I've got to get out of here. Fast. Help me up." Sim grabbed hold of my wrists and pulled me up. "Where can we go?'

Sim snapped his fingers. "I know just the place. There's both sun and shade. It's not that far from here. Can you make it," he asked mischievously, "or do I have to carry you?"

Had I the brain power to think out a reply, I would have laughed and threatened to take him up on it. As it was I nodded faintly, keeping my eyes fixed firmly on the ground. My hair fell in a dark curtain around my face, helping to shut out the sun. I took each step one at a time, as though I were afraid if I trod too hard the ground might give way beneath me.

Soon, the voice at the back of my mind whispered. *Soon the waiting will be over.*

I stumbled then and would've fallen, had not Sim been supporting me. The wind gusted, and I shivered.

The spot turned out to be on the cliffside. I felt a mild sense of surprise and pleasure. As promised, there was shade enough to hide in, and no sun in my eyes when I looked at the view. Sim stood tall, his back to me, looking out to sea himself.

For no reason that I could think of, I was tired to the point of exhaustion. I sagged back against the hard, but surprisingly smooth rock. Sim, on the other hand, was full of boundless energy, laughing and showing off for me. My headache was still very much with me, but Sim was at his entertaining best and kept me smiling most of the time.

This may have gone on for a half hour or more—time seemed irrelevant—when there came a moment of great stillness. Even the waves below seemed to hesitate in their rhythmic crashing. The seagulls stopped their crying, and the wind dropped off to nil. All of nature was holding its breath.

I held out my hands, and Sim took them, raising me to my feet as in some ballroom dance of old. Peace filled me. The time had come; the moment was now. We kissed. There were no firecrackers this time, set off by a careless child, or burst of gunfire from whatever movie we happened to be watching, or even rainbows. Just sudden and complete darkness.

I smiled, opening my eyes.

"Hey!" Sim's voice was higher than usual. "What's going on?"

"It's the eclipse," I told him calmly. I could feel the dread in him. Not fear exactly, just a natural abhorrence to that which was strange to him—the absence of light.

His body went rigid, and when I tried to step back, out of the circle of his arms, he wouldn't let me. "It's just the eclipse," I repeated. "Granted, it's a total one, but a few minutes from now it'll be all over. I rather like it myself."

"No, it won't," Sim said uneasily. Then he began shouting. I said nothing, keeping silent even when Sim lashed out at me. "Do you think I don't know? I read up on the subject the minute I heard we were having an eclipse, and I'm telling you it's not supposed to be like this. The sun's corona should give off more light for one thing, and the darkness should have come gradually, not just like that!" He snapped his fingers. "Like blowing out a candle! It's wrong. All wrong!" He drove his words home with angry emphasis.

For five minutes and then six we stood there in total silence. Well into the seventh I spoke. I said one word, "Catalyst," and felt all the blood drain slowly from my face. What had I done now? What *had* I done? Unforeseen disaster, the tarot had said. What could be more unforeseen that this?

This time I was the one to lead the way, guiding Sim around the rocks and tree roots on the trail. My exhaustion of before was gone, and my steps lively. I was in my element. The darkness was my friend just as the light had been my foe. My extrasensory instinct got us off the cliff face without a single misstep. The thought of the sheer drop below did not once cross my mind.

Sim and I separated without a word at the school, he heading for the bright lights, and I veering off into the darkness. The populace would be just beginning to figure out something had gone wrong, and I had no wish to be among them when the panic broke out—for the panic would come.

I ran in the darkness, feeling the rush of the wind through my hair. I might well have been alone in the whole of the universe, and its vastness embraced me. The corona that Sim had spoken of was dimly visible overhead, as the moon shines by night, only this was ring-shaped and missing the moon's usual cold, clear outline. The stars were shining few and faintly, almost as if they were being eclipsed as well.

I went back to the caravan to catch the evening news. Zsa met me at the door, face anxious, stepping back without a word when she saw it was me.

The dinner dishes still lay unwashed in the sink. All around there was an atmosphere of things being suddenly abandoned. It spoke of fear.

In silence, I switched on the TV and sat down to watch. Zsa hovered in the background, with that look of horrified knowing frozen on her face.

The TV maps were on again, with Lorelei this time circled in red. I smiled wryly. A week ago, Lorelei—with its population of slightly less than two thousand people—had been virtually unknown and equally unimportant. Now it had made the national news not once, but twice. The newsman seemed to think this significant because he again mentioned the lack of P and S waves in our recent earthquake as a lead into the bigger, more dramatic news of what the media began to call The Eclipse That Stuck. Of course, other towns and a 167-mile circle of country also lay in the moon's darkest inner shadow, the umbra, but Lorelei was in the exact centre of the circle.

The newsman didn't say a lot that I didn't already know. How could he, when Sim, Nancy Jean and I were the only ones who knew about the Catalyst—with the possible exception of Russell? All the network could do was show constant replays from every angle of what it looked like now, "live from Lorelei, British Columbia."

Mr. Hairspray himself interviewed two scientists who couldn't agree on anything. One said that An Eclipse That Stuck was a flat-out impossibility and accused the media as being "sensationalist." The other fellow went so far as to admit he had no idea "what in hell was going on."

They continued to give warnings not to look at the sun and reported three hospital admissions for possible blindness.

Various diagrams of solar eclipses and the rotation of the earth were shown, but no logical explanation was waiting to be found. What was happening here and now, to my mind, had little to do with logic.

Zsa had one thing to say to me. "Did you do it?"

I didn't bother to pretend I hadn't understood the question. "Yes." I got up and left then, shutting the door firmly on Zsa's still standing figure and on the noise from the TV. I headed straight for the Market to take my shift in the tent. I could see my breath in the air. The temperature was cooler than before, and dropping.

A large number of our regular customers came up, confused and seeking advice. All their questions dealt with the continuing darkness of the eclipse. One rotund lady, Mrs.

Kent, was so frightened she asked me if Judgment Day had befallen us. I let my eyes cross for a minute, then told her that was God's knowledge alone, but that I thought no. Not yet. That seemed to do the trick, and she scuttled away crablike, keeping well within the lighted area.

Russell came at about nine o'clock. I had been expecting him. I wondered how much he knew. He had probably run across Sim as well after the Chem explosion. Now to find our presence here again in Lorelei, where mysterious earthquakes occurred and total darkness reigned ... it was enough to give pause to the most skeptical of men.

"Hello, Medusa." He smiled in a deceptively friendly fashion and sat down across from me.

I didn't smile back or in any way acknowledge his presence.

He turned up the dimmer switch, causing my left eye to twitch jerkily. For a second he looked disconcerted, then he plunged right in. "You might remember me. I was the reporter waiting for you on the school steps in Clapton." He leaned forward. *"The day you blew up the Chemistry lab."* He paused expectantly.

I didn't so much as blink, neither confirming nor denying the accusation.

"In any case, I remember you. I nosed around at the school and had a cozy little chat with a former teacher of yours." Russell tried harder for a reaction. "A Mrs. Hopkins. Sound familiar?"

I was as still as a statue, but a small chill was beginning to creep up my spine. How much did he know?

"I had a hunch about you and decided to follow it up. After all, how often do school Chemistry labs blow up? Not very often," he said softly. "It took me awhile, tracking you on odd weekends and so forth, until I found you here. I had an interesting conversation with a friend of yours, one Nancy

Jean." He smiled smugly, holding up his notebook in a vague threat. "And then there was that business about the earthquake. Poor Ralph Barton. He was fool enough to get in your way, wasn't he?"

I fought off a strong urge to ask Russell what he thought he was doing if he wasn't getting in my way? And what exactly was there to prevent me from turning my powers on him? The anger in me was building.

Perhaps something showed in my eyes for Russell suddenly abandoned his previous method of baiting me and got right to the point. "And now we're having a permanent eclipse. The scientific world is stumped. But you and I know the truth, don't we? You're a Catalyst. Things happen around you—little 'accidents,' shall we call them?—just by your being there. Do you have any idea," Russell's self-centred face showed real excitement for the first time, "exactly how much money the right person would be willing to pay for one of your ... accidents ... in the right place at the right time?" His eyes glittered feverishly; I could almost see the dollar signs in them. "Money, lots and lots of money," he promised. "What you're doing now can hardly be raking in the cash." He looked around the tent in distaste.

My anger rushed to the fore. Who was he to criticize how I buttered my bread? I had no trouble staying still now. I was too still.

"So what do you say, kid?" Russell smiled recklessly. "Do you want to be rich?"

I was quiet for a long, long time until Russell began to get the fidgets. Then, very, very slowly I extended my hand palm up. "Cross my palm with silver and get your fortune told."

"Then you accept?" Delighted, Russell reached for my hand.

I kept my face expressionless. "Cross my palm with silver and get your fortune told."

For a moment the smile froze on Russell's ferret face, then he made a conscious effort to relax, saying in his best buddy-buddy tone, "In need of some cash, eh? No problem." He laid a crumpled bill in my hand.

I closed my eyes and began to moan softly under my breath. "Your name is David Russell. You were born in Vancouver. You have two older sisters by the names of Mary and Ruth. You drive a tan Chevy pick-up."

Russell forced a laugh. "Okay kid, I get the message. You've done your homework as well."

I ignored him, concentrating solely on the pain between my eyes. "You have two black marks for speeding on your driver's license. You had fish and chips for lunch yesterday and you didn't tip the waitress. You flunked your Grade 12 English final."

Russell was no longer laughing. "That's enough kid," he said testily. "You've made your point."

Oh, have I? I thought savagely. I'm not through with you yet. The best part is yet to come. "You owe money to someone called Vinny, and three days from now Vinny is going to catch you."

Russell looked ill, physically ill, like I'd punched him in the stomach. "How'd you know?" he gasped, then realizing how much he'd given away, smiled thinly. "Ha ha. Very funny, Medusa. You nearly had me going there for a minute with all that talk about loan sharks." Russell tripped himself in his own words.

I began to smile.

"Trying to make me toe the line, eh?" Russell snarled. "Well, it won't work. I've been playing these games a lot longer than you have. You aren't going to get rid of me that easily." His voice held a distinct trace of a whine.

My smile grew wider.

Little beads of sweat broke out on Russell's forehead. "You are joking, aren't you?" He was almost pleading now. "Three days?"

"No, Russell," I said ever so gently. "I never joke."

"How do I know you're not lying to me?" It was a last-ditch effort on Russell's part.

So I spelled it out for him. Clearly. "If the Vinny that you know has a scar on his neck about so long...." I demonstrated with my fingers. Russell paled even more, and I knew with a sudden burst of power that it was Russell who had put that scar there. And Vinny didn't strike me as the forgiving type.

Still he tried to bluff it out. "And if it is the Vinny I know?"

I smiled wickedly. "Why, then if I were you I'd leave town. Fast. He caught up with Franco last night," I pulled the name out of the air, but it had a surprising effect on Russell, who jackknifed up off the cushions barely waiting for me to finish my sentence, "and Franco squealed." Russell shot out of the tent like a bat out of hell, and left, gunning his tan Chevy pickup for all it was worth.

I could've told him not to bother. I had said three days, and I had meant three days.

Chapter Ten

Unto the Seventh Generation

I had the first dream that night. It was different than all my other ESP visions, first of all because of its extraordinary vividness. And secondly because it was about my mother.

I knew her on sight. Her facial features were easily recognizable when compared to mine, having the same cast of ugliness, only in her case they were more blurred and not as definite as mine. She was young yet and sat amid the drapings of a red-and-white circus tent while carousel music winged by. She was shuffling a deck of hand-painted tarot cards, fanning them out in one deft movement on the table before her and gathering them up again. She flipped one card over and became absolutely still. It was the most shocking of all the major arcana—the pale horse and its rider, Death.

Footsteps. Strange how they stood out so distinctly in the swarming crowd outside. Customers, yet my mother made no move to put away the cards, watching the door with intent eyes.

This was a young married couple, the type immediately obvious to anyone trained in people-watching. They were out for a lark, not really believing in the power of the fortune-teller, yet intrigued in spite of themselves. The woman had cotton candy stuck on her chin and a wide smile on her face.

"Cross my palm with silver and get your fortune told," my mother demanded in a voice hoarse with an accent. Her outstretched hand was rough and calloused beyond its years, nothing like the smooth pink of the cotton-candy lady's. I felt a brief rush of anger even in my role of dream observer. It wasn't fair: both women were about the same age.

The man was tall, blond, and perfectly at ease. He turned his head in a gesture I knew well. It was Sim's gesture. So this must be his father.

My mother stiffened at the same time, refusing to touch the two-dollar bill he offered.

"No?" He looked surprised. She remained stony-faced. Then, persuasively, "We really do want our fortune told." His hand went to his wallet again for a ten.

My mother looked at him contemptuously. The silence was thick for a moment. The woman—I now recognized her as Sim's mother about twenty years younger—plucked at his sleeve. She knew trouble when she saw it. "Perhaps we should just leave," she whispered. But her husband had a stubborn streak as well and slammed the money down. He returned Mama's stare blink for blink.

"So," Mama said at last, gathering up the ten. "You wish to have fortune told. I tell it. No," this when he extended a hand, "not yours. Hers."

Hesitantly, she held her hand out. Mama took it. No one could say she did not know her business; she fluttered the whites of her eyes and waited just the right amount of time. Her eyes, when she opened them, gleamed with malice. "You are Trevellyan." As she disregarded Sim's mother's gasp, Mama pointedly ignored the young man, but I could tell she was watching for his reaction out of the corner of her eyes. However, he was less impressed, arms folded across his chest, obviously reserving judgment.

Mama's eyes flashed resentment, and deliberately she went on to the more sensational news. "You will have baby soon." Another gasp from the young woman, this time mingled with shock at the audacity of the Gypsy woman. "A son. He will be born to you on the first day of the New Year." Mama bent her head over the palm now, looking deeper even as the frightened woman tried to snatch it away.

Now the trance had taken hold. "And I will have a daughter on the last day of the Old Year. And it is destined that the two shall meet. Great darkness will then fall upon the world, and all attendant evil."

Sim's mother was crying now, helpless tears, pulling in vain to get her hand back. "Dan, help me! I don't want to hear any more! Make her stop!"

He pried them apart, breaking the contact and ending the trance. The outraged young man started to hurry his sobbing wife away, but not before the last words drifted from the lips of the prophetess: "Unto the seventh generation."

I jerked awake then, to find myself huddled in the phone booth just outside of the Market, clad only in thin pajamas. I had no knowledge of getting there, but my quarter was paid, and my fingers were already dialling feverishly. I pressed the frozen earpiece to my ear. Only when the phone began to ring did I realize I didn't know what number I had dialled.

"Hello?" said the voice on the other end with a hint of annoyance.

"Hello," I returned politely, hanging on to my patience. "Could I speak to Sim, please?"

"Just a min—" The voice sharpened suddenly. "Who's calling?" I could sense the fear behind Sim's mother's question. Not even in my own mind could I call her Mrs. Trevellyan.

"This is Medusa."

The receiver slammed down in my ear. Very slowly I hung up. I could now understand her pallor and shock when she first came upon me and Sim kissing. Mine was not a forgettable face. No doubt she had connected me instantly with the fortuneteller who had given her the dire warning.

I didn't bother to phone back, but fifteen minutes later when Sim's red car pulled up I was dressed and waiting. I got in wordlessly and we zoomed off, the headlights cutting through the dark. Patches of ice were beginning to form where yesterday there were puddles.

"You had the dream, too." I stated a fact. For a moment it seemed Sim wouldn't even answer. Then he gave the briefest of nods, flooring the gas pedal so that the speedometer edged up to 120.

Personally, speeds do nothing for me other than raise the hair on the back of my neck. I hung on for as long as I could before suggesting to Sim that he slow down. "Or else we're going to end up stranded out in the middle of nowhere."

He obligingly slowed and pulled onto the side of the road. I kept quiet while he stared straight ahead, wrestling in his mind for the right way to begin. After what seemed a full minute, he broke the silence.

"Do they always come like that?" Sim turned from the windshield to me, still gripping the steering wheel with both hands. "So sudden and overpowering?"

"Always," I said, surprised. "Don't you know?" I had been so positive that he possessed the Gift as well.

He shrugged. "Little flashes here and there. Never anything I could actually grasp."

And so he had ignored them; I could read it in his eyes. A typical reaction. People didn't like the unknown, and so they pretended it didn't exist. "But you could grasp this one," I stated. The memory of my own vision was still with me. I had not been strictly truthful when I'd said visions were all alike—this one *had been* different, more powerful and carrying a great deal more impact.

"It scared the hell out of me," Sim stated baldly, causing me to look askance at his face. He gave the ghost of a laugh. "There I was, in my own living room having a bang-up fight with Dad over—well, never mind what—and then Whammo! I'm not there anymore. I'm at some fleabag circus I've never seen before, with—get this—my twenty-year-old parents. Only I'm not really there ... I don't have a body, and as far as Mom and Dad are concerned, I haven't been so much as thought of."

Sim's voice, which had been rising, ground to a halt, his knuckles white on the steering wheel. My heart squeezed for him. The dream had been a little overwhelming, even for me, and Sim had practically had no firsthand experience with the supernatural.

The darkness crowded in against me then, and I heard myself say as if from a great distance away, "Better get used to it. There are six more to come." Then I was back in the car again and Sim was looking at me with horrified eyes.

"You *are* her daughter, aren't you?"

"Yes." Oddly enough, his question pleased me. I sensed that he thought the Gypsy woman ugly, but that he no longer thought of me the same way.

Another silence. Then, "I asked Dad about it, you know."

"And?"

"And it's all true. Mom was pretty shaken, demanding how I knew. I had to say you'd told me. Hope you don't mind."

"Not a bit." There was little else left to say.

Sim drove me home shortly afterward, kissing me rather hard before leaving.

The eclipse was still fixed firmly in the sky when Zsa awoke me the next morning. Her face looked pinched and breakfast had lost its usual flavour. The radio was on, but after the news clip on the fourth robbery, Zsa shut it off rather abruptly, nearly twisting off the knob in the process. She muttered something in Romanee that I didn't quite catch; and her eyes, when they rested on me, held something suspiciously close to fear.

Zsa, afraid of me? I shook my head as if to clear it. Nonsense. But I didn't convince myself. I had seen enough fear on the faces of others to know what it looked like. Without saying good-bye, I stepped out of the motorhome into decidedly colder weather.

The whole day had a feeling of unreality, as if everyone was trying to convince themselves that this wasn't really happening. It couldn't be. It was too ... too unbelievable. Less than half the students had shown up, and more left at noon. Those who were there slipped from classroom to classroom like ghosts, saying little above a whisper, making a pretense of working. And always, always, they looked out the windows, eyes drawn to the darkness. Even Nancy Jean's cheerfulness did not quite ring true.

It wasn't until after school that things got sticky. A media horde was waiting at the doors wanting a "young person's opinion" on what was happening. The response was not as good as you might have thought. Even within the bright circle of TV lights the students felt naked, unprotected, and it showed in their expressions. Most offered incoherent half-sentences or no comment. The Sim I had met at the Valentine's Dance, however, was a natural for TV, and the reporters were quick to pick up on that, thrusting half a dozen mikes under his nose.

I faded quietly into the background, wanting just to watch, but Sim grew less and less at ease. He began to answer their questions in short, sharp sentences and his eyes searched the crowd somewhat wildly. *For me.* Joy washed through me and I stood just a little straighter, repeating the words under my breath, "For me."

When I got home it was to find Zsa propped up in front of the TV like some kind of zombie. She didn't look up when I sat down beside her just gave me the report. "It's growing."

My mood of peace shattered. "What's growing?" I asked, but I already knew the answer.

"The darkness," Zsa said in that same dead tone of voice. "Yesterday it only went as far as Clapton, now it's just outside Vancouver. People are going crazy, Medusa." She caught my eye for the first time, pleading. "They're abandoning their houses ... even their families, driving all night long just to keep ahead of the darkness. It's a disaster. They've even had the prime minister come on the news cautioning everyone to stay where they are and not panic. It's only darkness after all. Isn't it, Medusa? Isn't it?" Zsa grabbed me by the shoulders and started to shake me.

Normally such a thing would have enraged me, but with the darkness came some measure of control. In any case I was trancing out again.

This dream was of my Grandmother. She too was easily recognizable when compared to my mother, but a shade less ugly, with normal dark-lashed eyes. She was at approximately the same stage of life that my mother had been in the dream before, twentyish, but wearing the married head scarf of the Gypsy.

When it was over I knew neither more nor less than before. Grandmother had been raised an orphan as well and had only the quotation, "Unto the seventh generation," to go on. She knew also that she was fifth in a line of all girls. She wept when her own daughter was born. The curse would continue. And it had continued ... until now it rested on me.

It was on the third day of darkness that the doomsayers appeared, grim misfits carrying placards and signs, begging us to repent, that the Day of Judgment was upon us. Ironically, the crime rate was still jumping—break-ins, muggings, and inexplicable acts of violence. There was at least one siren in the air whenever you stopped to listen.

Sim was oddly serious that day, refusing to discuss the dreams other than to say that yes, he had had one as well. School had been cancelled indefinitely, and I was on edge as we drove around looking for some of the gang. He looked to be losing his tan, and the nervousness he had exhibited the second day had increased rather than worn off. He was too quick to laugh and too soon to stop.

By the fourth day, the eclipse that scientists had scoffed at was rapidly becoming a world concern. All regular programming was pre-empted to provide twenty-four hour coverage of the "bizarre event." Weathermen suddenly had something to get excited about and developed elaborate theories about descending convective air masses. The effects of no sunlight were beginning to intensify as plants began to die and the thermometer kept up its downward plunge. Strangely enough, the reports of eye damage stopped pouring in as people stopped paying attention to that aspect of the eclipse.

But what was most unsettling to the nation, the dark spot had continued to grow with Lorelei at its very centre.

As the dreams continued and the days in the moon's shadow wore on, things seemed only to improve for me. Headaches were a thing of the past, regardless of how many lights they turned on inside. My temper was down to a manageable level, and I even managed to catch up on some of my schoolwork.

I took an active pleasure in the dreams, filling in the blanks of my family history as they drew me back, back, back into time. Each one added a detail, either about me or the accursed web that spanned the generations. Dispassionate, yet involved, I looked forward to the next revelation.

I would have been more than content to let the eclipse remain forever if it hadn't been for one thing, and that one thing happened to be what I cared about most in the world. Sim.

He was losing weight as well as colour, and now it was almost an effort for him to smile at my feeble attempts at humour. He was unused to it, never having been sick a day before in his life, and the dark depressed him. He didn't say so. How could he after I had endured the light for years and this was only his fifth day? I could read it in his face as plain as day, no pun intended.

It was on this fifth day that it happened. We were at Nancy Jean's and the phone rang. Nothing so terrible about that, was there? And yet both Sim and I waited with baited breath while, with what seemed to be agonizing slowness, Nancy Jean went to answer the phone.

She waited for another ring. "Hello? Yes, he's right here. Hang on a sec." She covered the mouthpiece with her hand and went to holler, but Sim was already standing there, waiting to take it.

The expression on his face—expectancy and fear—scared me. My throat went suddenly dry. Something was wrong. I knew it. Sim's next words confirmed it. "Mother? Is it ... ? I'm coming right away!" He dropped the phone like a hot coal and made a dash for the door. I leapt up just as quickly and followed him out, leaving Nancy Jean standing open-mouthed in her hallway.

I threw myself onto the car seat beside Sim, my door not even closed as we shot away from the curb. The journey was a short swift one, with Sim screeching and skidding around corners, totally ignoring all traffic laws, the ice, and any other vehicle unfortunate enough to be on the road at the same time. Not once did he look my way, though he must have known I was there with him in the car. We parked in front of a low white building and Sim jumped out, abandoning the keys in the ignition. It was only as I went through the white doors myself that I realized we were in the hospital.

I got there in time to see Sim put his arms around his mother and hear her sobbing. "You know he wasn't feeling well, but he insisted on going to work anyhow, and today, at around noon, he just ... just collapsed!" Sim's mother was weeping buckets. "He's in a coma and the doctors don't know how long ... how long...."

"Shhh. It's all right. There, there." Sim patted her back awkwardly. A nurse steered them to a room marked "Family Admittance Only."

I stayed standing exactly where I was, in the middle of the main hallway, mindless of the disinfectant smell around me and the nurse's pointed glances. Now at last I understood—the sickness, the nerves, everything. My forehead was burning, and I pressed it against the cold stone wall. My mother had been right to name me Medusa, the accursed.

My mouth firmed. There was no sense in self-pity; there were things to do and I had best get on with them ... before it really was too late. I went directly from the hospital to the Market and told Zsa and Leo what had to be done. To my surprise Leo did not want to leave, a stubborn look coming over his swarthy face. "We have good job here."

My features turned to rock. "We must leave." Madame Rosa had given me the power to command and I was using it now.

By the sixth day the arrangements had been made, the fortunetelling tent dismantled and the caravan ready to roll. We were leaving and hopefully the darkness would leave with us.

Leo turned the ignition and, after a few false starts, the motor began to throb. My face felt unnaturally stiff and I stared stonily straight ahead. Hurry, I willed Leo. Hurry before ... but I did not know what to hurry for.

Honkkkkk! The noise came from outside, and my heart jolted painfully against my ribs when I realized its source. There, caught in the beam of our headlights, was a red sports car. Its occupant leapt out and tore across the road, blond hair reflecting white. It was Sim.

I made no sign, remaining perfectly still in the shadows, but still he found me, choosing the right door to the right motorhome without hesitation. "Medusa!" he gasped, out of breath, "What do you think you're doing?"

"I'm leaving," I stated, keeping my eyes trained out the windshield. *What does it look like I'm doing?* I screamed at him silently.

"Why?" was his next question.

I closed my eyes as if in pain. How could he ask that? How could he, when it was for his sake I was leaving?

"I love you," were his next words.

The words froze me.

Love.

I had never allowed myself to so much as consider the word. Love was for poets and beautiful Southern belles, not for me. Not for Medusa, the ugly, the hideous. That straightened my head. It was inconceivable, of course, that he loved me. Who, after all, had? Ever?

Suddenly shaking with rage, I turned and faced him. "Don't you say that!" I yelled. "Don't you say that to me!"

Sim's face was the whitest I'd ever seen it and he let several seconds of absolute silence go by before replying, "Who would you rather I say it to?"

That finished me. For the first time in my life that I could remember I began to cry. And cry and cry. I talked as well, in between the tears, blaming myself. The darkness was my fault. I even liked it, and now his father was in the hospital, and it was killing him.

And all the while Sim held me, comforting me, finishing with, "I'm not so easy to kill off as all that and neither's my Dad. A little dark never hurt anyone." Still, his smile was noticeably thin and he looked drained.

I straightened abruptly. "You ought to be there with your mother. She needs you."

"Yes, I suppose she does." He sighed and raked his fingers through his hair. I noticed with alarm the circles under his eyes and drooping shoulders. I volunteered to drive him down. The fact that he agreed showed just how tired he really was. Sim never let anyone drive his car.

I had little to worry about in the way of explanation to Zsa and Leo. They had faded into the background and began unpacking the minute Sim burst in our door.

The sixth dream was, inevitably, six generations back down the line. This girl—the dream showed her to be of no more than nine or ten years old—was not in the least ugly, just plain, and she lived back in the Old Country in Europe. She lived with her Grandfather in a cart pulled by two scrawny oxen and their home was wherever they happened to be when the oxen stopped, be it a few feet away from last night's camp or ten miles. On some days the oxen would not start out, no matter how hard Grandfather hit them, and these days that was not very hard at all. Grandfather was dying.

For many days she had guessed as much and been afraid, but today, for the first time, Grandfather admitted it himself. Today he was too weak to get out of bed. He called her over so that she knelt beside him and spoke in Romanee. "I am dying, my child. No, no tears." He brushed her cheek feebly. "You must listen to me. I will be gone soon and there are things I must tell you. Your mother," he paused solemnly, "would have wished it so."

The tears stopped. She was interested in spite of her sorrow. Many times before, she had asked about her mother, but Grandfather would not tell her, saying it would keep until a later day. Perhaps this later day had finally arrived.

"There is a man who wishes to find you. He is a cruel, wicked man, and you must run from him. His name is Trevellyan just as yours is."

The words burned themselves into my brain, even as I observed in the dream. How could this be? I, a Trevellyan?

The girl's brow knotted into a frown and, just for a moment, she resembled me. "Why must I run? Perhaps he has repented and wants to help us. Perhaps—"

"No, Miranda!" Grandfather's voice was agitated and he struggled to sit up. "Do not go to him for help! He has cursed you and yours even unto the seventh generation!"

Then he died and I heard only Miranda's pitiful whimper of "Grandfather!" before the dream was replaced by reality.

The darkness by now had spread almost all around the globe. One more day and it was expected to envelope the whole of the world. Dire predictions of the end of the world increased tenfold on radio and TV, with CNN setting the expiration date for tomorrow.

Sim's father was still in critical condition, and I had just gotten to the hospital that afternoon when I felt it. Not a pinprick, or a small shudder along my ESP nerves, but a full-fledged blow. I fell to the floor under the force of it, picked myself up and began to sprint.

Sim. I chanted his name under my breath. Sim, please be okay. Don't die, Sim! Please!

I navigated the halls at a flat-out run, slicing through the crowd to where Sim lay. His eyes were closed and his face bloodless, but he was alive. I had to clutch the wall for a second for my own support, and the group of orderlies and nurses closed me out. They were already strapping him onto a stretcher and wheeling him down the hallway. The door was shut in my face and, now when I needed it the most, my authority-defying anger seemed to have deserted me, leaving me numb with fear.

A nurse told me to please go to the waiting room, but I refused to budge, clinging to whatever was nearest.

Sim's mother arrived then, eyes haunted as if she had been expecting this for a long, long time now. Only when she saw me did she turn hysterical, demanding at a pitch a little lower than a shriek, "What's *she* doing here? Who let her in here?" She began to sob, beating at me with her fists. "You did this! You're killing them. You're evil, that's what! Evil!"

I stayed perfectly still, letting her accusations rain down upon me. My left eye began to jerk around in its socket, a tell-tale sign of aroused anger. But it was not her I was angry at, nor did I blame myself.

I left the hospital then and found myself a dark place between a large garbage bin and the loading dock where I could hide and wait. Soon the dream would come and I'd be able to act. Only the dreams knew the whole story. And today was the seventh day. There was still yet time.

The seventh dream was again different, spanning a lifetime in a kaleidoscope of flashing pictures, instead of just a short piece of it. It started off like a fairy tale.

Once upon a time there was a beautiful Gypsy girl. She had the Gift and made but one mistake—she fell in love with the handsome son of the local Baron. They became engaged, and plans for the wedding were made.

His name was Richard; hers, Lorelei. Lurer to the rocks.

Enter the villain, in the shape of Richard's father, Baron Guy Trevellyan. He had been away at the time of the engagement and was furious to arrive home and find his only son marrying someone of "bad blood." Part of his journey had been to arrange a marriage between Richard and the daughter of a neighbouring Count. She was of the aristocracy and had a sizable dowry as well.

The Baron did all he could, using his influence to delay matters through the Church and threatening to disinherit Richard if he did not stop seeing the girl immediately. Richard refused and the couple eloped. In a fit of anger Guy disowned Richard and gave orders he be thrown off the estate should he ever return.

Lorelei's father disapproved as well, warning that such a match could only end in great pain for both of them.

Richard had his inheritance from his mother, and for a time the young couple lived happily. Then the dream changed, turned sinister.

Word of a war, carried by an ill wind, came their way. Baron Trevellyan was under attack and Richard rode off to help. He laughed at Lorelei's fears and "silly superstitions." Of course he would be coming back. See if he didn't. And so one night he went, leaving Lorelei staring into the embers of a dying fire. She was very pregnant by this time, and travel was difficult. I could feel her despair and sense of great loss.

Guy Trevellyan himself brought the news. "He's dead, killed in battle." Still she sat staring into space, and after one look Guy became incensed, "But you already knew that, didn't you?" He grabbed her by the shoulders and began to shake her. "Didn't you? You knew he was to die and yet you sent him to his death!" He slapped her hard across the face. Despite his grief I could see the enjoyment and hatred in his face, and it made me sick. This, then, was where my black rages originated. From Guy Trevellyan himself.

There were tears running down Lorelei's cheeks now and her whispered "Yes" spoke of intolerable pain.

"You'll pay for this. I swear you will. If it were not for Richard's son that you are carrying I'd kill you right now." He set guards outside the door, but she was not without friends and they helped her escape during the night.

The Baron found her, of course, barging in even as she lay dying. The hut was little more than a hovel and he looked around at its humble furnishings with contempt. "Gone back to your beginnings, I see." She made no reply and he rapidly got down to business. "Where is the boy?"

"Boy? What makes you think there is a boy?" Lorelei tried to bluff, but the fear showed all too plainly on her face.

A cry, muffled too late, was heard from the next room. In two strides he pushed through the curtain. The child kicked and screamed, but the Baron held him easily under his arm like a bag of potatoes.

"No!" Lorelei reached for her son instinctively, only to be pushed back down with the Baron's free hand, her eyes glazed with pain and hate.

Dispassionately, he surveyed her, fallen and dying. "So the good Tinker's curse worked after all."

"Curse! Pah!" Even in her weakness the Gypsy managed to convey her contempt. "What know you of curses?" she wheezed between breaths.

His jaw tightened and for a moment I thought he would strike her, but he regained control of himself. "Not a thing. That's why I let one of your own kind do it. He even threw in a mother-to-daughter curse that will follow you even unto the seventh generation."

Lorelei was slipping fast, yet a certain light came into her dark eyes. "You think it is so easy to divide light from dark, good from evil? The time will come when there will be light where there is now dark, and dark where there was once light!" It was my future she was seeing, and I peered with her into its depths. But, in so saying, she died.

It was not until years later that the Baron found out that Lorelei had borne twins and that the Gypsy's daughter still lived. In a rage he sent men to seek out and kill her, but he need not have bothered. The curse had begun its work.

I opened my eyes to darkness and got up, purpose in my movements. The dream had shown me the way. It was my Catalytic powers that had brought on the eclipse, and so it was up to me to undo it as well. And the task must be done now before Sim could stop me. Moving with calm efficiency I left my corner—walking, not running—to the cliffside where Sim and I had sat to watch the eclipse.

Here there were no artificial lights to disturb me, and I could do what I had to do. I felt no fear. I had known this moment was coming ever since the day long ago when I saw, for the first and last time, Sim's house.

I stood alone for a moment and all was silent. Again the waves seemed to hold their breath as I took one last look around me, memorizing each seam and crack in the cliff-face beside me, the sandy shore and broken rocks below. Ice crystals sparkled in the air. My eyes lifted upwards.

The sun's corona flared brightly against the pitch-black sky. Light where there was dark and dark where there was once light.

I looked directly at it and visions began to flash before my eyes. The Gypsy-dark and Saxon-blond heads of Lorelei and Richard ... Miranda and her twin ... my grandmother and Mama ... Sim's parents ... and finally Sim.

He was sitting bolt upright in his hospital bed, his blue eyes wide with horror. There was a nurse at the foot of his bed, checking the charts and scolding him, but he didn't see her. His eyes stared straight into mine, voice hoarse. "No, Medusa! Don't. There has to be a better way."

Sadly, I could say nothing back. This was the only way. The tarot had said so, and my vision had foretold it. My eyes did not waver, fixed on the golden halo of the heavens.

At first the moon remained a black disc in the centre. And then oh-so-slowly it began to move, very slightly, off to the right.

The light didn't hurt, not at first, and I kept my gaze steadily locked on the emerging sun. The moon moved some more, allowing a full crescent of the sun to come into view. That's when the pain started, making my eyes overflow with tears. Still I watched, until the orb of the sun emerged fully into the sky and the image of the eclipse was burnt into the retina of my eye.

I didn't know when to stop watching because, within me, all was dark. I was blind.

An eighth vision filled my mind. It was of sunshine and spring. Children's voices laughed and shouted as they were pushed higher and higher on the swing. Blond and dark heads played together happily, sharing toys.

The curse was broken. My children, the eighth generation, would be free. As I was now. Never again would I get migraines from the presence of light, nor would I explode in anger. Never again would the Catalyst—now reversed—be allowed to hurt those nearest to me.

I could have gone on up the rocks and back home, or to the hospital. I would not have run into any walls. My Second Sight took care of that. Instead, I chose to stay where I was, basking in the warmth of the sun, waiting to be found.

After all, Sim always knew where I was.

The End

About Nicole Luiken

Photo by CINDY LANTI

Nicole Luiken was born May 25, 1971. She grew up on a farm near Manning, Alberta, but began to read and write at an early age. She wrote her first book at the age of thirteen and has never looked back.

She has written fourteen book-length manuscripts (probably more by the time you read this) and has two books in print besides this one: *Escape to the Overworld,* a science-fiction story, and *Unlocking the Doors,* a ghost story.

Although she wrote *The Catalyst* in Grade 10, it remains her favourite. The idea for this Teenage Psychic Adventure Romance was formed when Nicole "got sick and tired of reading about beautiful characters who were trying to choose between two or more boyfriends." As a result she created Medusa Noire, who is not only downright ugly, but cursed. What's more, Medusa has extrasensory perception and a violent temper.

Nicole graduated from high school with honours and is presently enrolled in a Library and Information Management course at Grant MacEwan College in Edmonton. In 1989, she won the YTV Youth Achievement Award in the category of Writing.

More Great Books from Tree Frog!

ESCAPE TO THE OVERWORLD

By Nicole Luiken — 144 pages

ISBN 88967-078-1 — $7.95pb

Grade Thirteen wasn't particularly lucky for Greg Matheson. One day he's a normal high school student complaining about his chemohydrate teacher, the next he's a prisoner of the Humanoids far below the surface of the earth. Recovering from psychosurgery, Greg meets Carmen, born of the Underground, and together they launch a campaign against the diabolical world-repopulation experiment being conducted by their robotic captors. Written by a prolific fifteen-year-old who dreams up her plots on the school bus, this teenage sci-fi adventure romance is a captivating look at technology gone wrong in a Toronto 200 years in the future.

I'LL TELL YOU TUESDAY IF I LAST THAT LONG

By Cherylyn Stacey — 144 pages

ISBN 88967-064-1 — $6.95pb

Being dumped in the middle of a thousand teenagers at a California teen beach and told "to have a good time" was *not* Vicky Delorian's idea of a good time. Neither, for that matter, was being taken on her mother's honeymoon. The alternative was staying with Margaret, her dreadful new aunt. These days Vicky's life was one problem after another. But when she caught the eye of Blake, who liked his girls young and dumb, she was about to find out what problems *are.* This striking first novel deals with wit and understanding about drug abuse, family problems, and the heart of a 14-year-old year girl.

IT SEEMED LIKE A GOOD IDEA AT THE TIME

By Martyn Godfrey — 112 pages

ISBN 88967-060-9 — $6.95pb

New to Edmonton, Mike Hughes is discovered by Jaws Williamson and Moose Podanski while the moving van is still unloading. Jaws has big plans for himself on the staff of next year's school newspaper. If he can only get the scoop on Judy Turner's all-girl party, he is sure he will be appointed editor. This is where Mike comes in. Jaws's fast tongue convinces him he must dress up as a girl and attend the party. And when Mike falls in love with Judy Turner, chaos results. "Martyn Godfrey is at his breeziest and funniest in this latest romp, very much in the spirit of the Ms. Teeny Wonderful book," enthuses *Children's Book News.*